Trigger Wa
BODY HORROR

Also by Madness Heart Press

Trigger Warning
Trigger Warning: Body Horror

Standalone
Creeping Corruption Anthology

Free Her

Maxine Kollar

Maxine Kollar is a wife and a mother of three. Her fiction, creative non-fiction and poetry have appeared online, in rear view mirrors and on tree trunks. Her works have recently appeared in print anthologies from Grivante Press, Pole to Pole Publishing, Wild Woman Medicine Circle, Schreyer Ink and Millhaven Press.

The girl wished her feet wouldn't do that. There were times when they would get so long that they would burst right out of her shoes. The whole foot would elongate a bit, but it was the way the toes not only lengthened but got a bit curly and big at the tips. She wore flip flops mostly, but that was not a perfect either. In the winter, people would give her strange looks even though it never became so cold that she was in any real danger. Still, it was better than having all of her shoes ruined and having to throw them out in the dumpster behind the apartment building. There were sometimes good things in that dumpster, but she could never remember what only the warm satiated feeling of being tucked down under layers like soft, warm blankets. She would only go in after tossing in her old shoes and just to double check she hadn't left any money in them. The gleaming coins in the front of her loafers had beckoned her in that first time.

The thing with her feet had another facet that was a bit more troubling. Her toenails get longer which was fun because she would paint faces on them that winked and giggled at her. That was okay when it happened at home but in class was a different story. She would tuck her feet under her desk when they started to grow, but the toenails would scrape along the tile and make that horrible sound. The class would pretend they didn't hear it, but she still cringed. She started humming to try and cover up the awful noise, but the mean girl next to her would look cross and give her quick, shh.

She really wanted to pay attention in class, but it was getting harder. Her ears were doing strange things. They would get pointy then floppy and do all kinds of weird things. There was no way to know what they were going to do next. This was a real bother, but they still worked well enough. Actually, they seemed like they worked better. She could hear people talking from far away, and that was okay except for when they were talking about her. This made her feel bad and made her want to cover her ears. She wanted one of those winter hats with the ear flaps, but she had to order it off the internet because there were none in the stores where she lived. She was so happy when it came in the mail. There were still some strange looks cast her way but the whispers stopped, or maybe she couldn't hear them anymore. That was alright in her book.

At first, it was just her feet that would get hairy when they grew, but now her legs were getting hairy too. She was shaving them four or five times a day to keep up. Her roommates started complaining about how she was monopolizing the bathroom, but there was nothing she could do about that. The bathtub was getting clogged, but they weren't complaining, so she didn't mention it, so she just started shaving her legs in the sink. The depression along her shin made her have to dig in with the razor and sometimes blood would rush to the surface, but she was persistent. Tiny hairs would sprout up with blood and would have to dig in to shave them out, but too soon the sink would fill up with the tiny hairs and the blood and run over onto the floor. The hairy red pool reminded her of menstrual blood and she swirled her fingers in it. It might have tasted good, but the sink was so close to the toilet that it must have mixed with drunken misses from one of her roommates. She withdrew her fingers from her mouth quickly but not before the taste acquired her. She sat on the floor, just one dip per finger she promised herself.

She wore pants mostly, but they had to be the really big kind because the hair would grow back so fast and stick out through the fabric, even denim. Big pants were good anyway because sometimes her stomach would grow so big that she needed the extra room. This wasn't too embarrassing because she just looked pregnant. She was young to be pregnant, but no one thinks anything about that kind of stuff anymore. She would lean way back and stick out her belly. People would look at it of course because it had to be a twenty-pound baby she was carrying and you hardly ever saw those. The belts kept popping when her stomach grew, so she just started using a length of rope around her waist. With the rope, she could just keep winding it around and around herself. It felt safe and snag, and she would wind it around her neck some-times, not for any harm to be sure, but just for the delicious snugness.

At the telemarketing office is where she first noticed that her hands were getting longer and hairier too. There were low walls around the little cubicles, so she didn't let that one bother her too much. Typing the info into the computer was getting very hard though. The finger-nails were so sharp and pointy that they kept slipping off the keys and she had to ask people to repeat their credit card numbers all the time. The people who monitor the calls kept telling her to pay more atten-tion but never mentioned her hands, but she still wanted to cover them. Even those stretchy gloves couldn't contain her hands when they start-ed to grow, and the fingernails would cut right through the knit fabric anyway. Oven mitts were a pretty good solution, the very thick padded kind. Putting duct tape around the wrists kept them from sliding off.

Talking was getting to be a real problem. Her teeth, some of them were getting very long and pointy too. She had to drop her jaw to try and hide those teeth. Trying to pronounce her words very slowly and clearly was hard, but she was doing her best. People would have to turn their heads to the side to try and hear her clearer. Licking her tongue over her teeth was the best she could do to clean them. Every time she tried to brush her teeth, the toothbrush would crumble against her sharp teeth.

She would have been more upset about not getting to brush her teeth, but she wasn't actually eating that much. She tried the donuts and the cakes and the pretzels, and the chip but they all tasted so ...fake. She remembered reading that single ingredient foods were so much better for you anyway. She took the package of ground beef out of the fridge and tried a small bite. That tasted real. That tasted right. She was so hungry that she ate the whole package. She knew she would get in trouble with the room-mate that it belonged to, but she was so hungry.

There was a fight she overheard her room-mates having one night about beer, and it devolved into so much shouting and cursing that she stuck her oven mitts over her ears and eventually crept down to the dumpster. So much distress over drinks left her shaken and determined to avoid refrigerated beverages any kind. There were a few degrees of separation, but when the wheel in her head spun toward the menstrual cup, she knew she had found her holy grail, and she cried and kissed it every night for twenty-one days. The taste of her own yellow stream had left her disgusted at her previous palette as she hovered over the coffee mug to prepare the ambrosia. She sipped with closed eyes and heaving breasts for seven days and then replaced the challis at the altar she had built. She would only spare a dram from the cup to mark this amazing occasion on the wall, but very soon the swirls lead her around and down paths that spiraled into writhing dances with a lover just beyond her knowing but well within her reach.

They asked her not to come into work anymore. She understood. It was tough to type with the oven mitts on, and it was so hard to get people to listen to her closely enough. She was asked to repeat herself all the time, and it was getting frustrating. She would put the earpiece under her hat so she could hear them well, but that wasn't good enough she guessed. They didn't mention the scraping toenails, but she suspected that the old lady in the cubicle next to hers had complained. She was always peeking over the low wall at her. They also did not mention the coarse hair on her legs sticking right through the pants and ripping up the chair fabric. She thought that was really decent of them. She just packed up her things and left. Everyone watched her go with so much intensity that she was sure they would regret their decision and call her back soon.

The same reasons she was asked to leave work were the same reasons she stopped going to class. The oven mitts made it hard to take notes, and the scraping toenails made everyone sit away from her, but at least they were nice about it. The other students would keep pretending to take notes even though she knew the scraping was so loud that no one could hear what the professor was saying. Most of the students but not that mean girl. No, she perpetually looked like she smelled cabbage but after reading the article about 'resting bitch face,' the girl decided not to take it personally. Still, she wondered if the mean girl would struggle long if she took her to the dumpster. She fantasized so much about catching her in the parking garage and taking her out behind the apartment building and getting naked and piercing her neck with the blade and letting the warm blood wash over her that it almost seemed real. She laughed at herself when she went finally went out there to check. The garbage truck had already come, and the dumpster was empty save for the ubiquitous brown stains.

Her room-mates were trying to get her to leave too. The hairs were ripping up the couch, and the stuffing from her bed and pillow floated all through the house now, making everyone cough. They said she might feel better if she took a shower like they didn't know her leg hairs clogged the drain weeks ago.

One of her room-mates had called the mother. The mother came there and cried and cried. Maybe the parents were getting a divorce or perhaps they were not happy with her grades. Oh, the mother would not stop crying; she was so sad. The girl, desperate to help, took off her belt and wound the length of rope around and around the mother's neck until she stopped crying. That was better. She put the mother in her footlocker so she could rest.

She woke up one night with her knees really bothering her. Rubbing them was no relief until she got up out of bed and rubbed more; with silky crunches and soothing cracks they slowly bent, and she crumbled to the floor. That felt really good. She folded herself down and put her hands on the floor. She could run around the room so fast and even up the walls now. She felt so free and alive.

The father called and wanted to know where the mother was. What did he care? He was probably cheating on her. Maybe that's why she was so sad and crying. He had no right to demand to know where she was. She told him she didn't know where the mother was, but he came anyway. He was sad and cried too, but the girl took no pity. She wanted to get away from him, but he told her to stay in the room and stood in front of the door... She was so mad that she bent her knees backward and ran all around the room and even up the walls. The father was so upset by what he did to the mother that he put his hand on his chest and fell asleep. The girl came down from the walls and put him in her footlocker to rest with the mother. At least they were together for a little while longer.

She loved bending her knees backward and running around her room at night. But one night, after accidentally knocking a few things over, one of the room-mates knocked at the door. She let the room-mate in. He began coughing immediately. He had never been inside her room before. What did he want? Did he want to hurt her or abuse her or kill her? He was talking about getting help with problems. Was she the problem? Was someone coming to help him with her? She was so afraid. What would she do if someone came and there were two of them? She had to get rid of one of them. She waited until he went over to the window and opened it. He bent so far out of the window and began to throw up that it was easy for her to push him out.

She settled down to sleep in her new bed. It was her old bed, but she had pulled out so much of her hair, leg hairs included, that she could make her bed really soft now. When she saw soft things on the sidewalk, she would pick them up and bring them home for her bed. The girl felt really good about this because she was cleaning the sidewalk, recycling and making her bed. She slept really well in her bed that night. Before morning she went down to the alley to help the room-mate who fell through the window. She helped him to the dumpster behind the building and left him with the brown stains and banana peels. A piece of broken glass sends her back to his throat, but the liquid is slow and thick and cold. Disappointed, she presses crinkles her face, like the mean girl from class, and walks away.

She knew she had to keep her knees locked forward when she was out and about in the daytime. It was hard now that she knew how good it felt to have them bent backward and she stumbled and fell a lot, but she realized that if she just pretended that she was drunk, then people would not look at her in that funny way. When night-time came, she would sneak out while she was supposed to be sleeping and run in the park with her knees bent back and her hands on the ground. The animals would play tag with her for a while, but they were so fast that she would just get frustrated and go back home.

On the girl's last walk outside, she sees a squirrel. It is plump and fat and moves so slowly that she thinks she might be able to catch it. She runs into the woods after it and chases it for quite some time. It is faster than it seemed at first. She starts getting hot and has to pull off the oven mitts, and she steps out of the flip flops. Slipping out of the pants, whipping off the hat and then the sweater is such a relief. Finally naked now, finally free now she can bend her knees back and run on her hands. So much faster now, she catches up to the fat brown squirrel, pulls up the brown fur and buries her teeth in the white belly. Funny sounds it makes.

They descend out of nowhere and pin her to the ground. Knees dig into her back, and dry leaves enter her gaping, disbelieving mouth.

Maybe it was just a park and not the woods, but it was just a squirrel. Why is everyone screaming?

Familiar Faces

Jeremy Megargee

Jeremy Megargee has always loved dark fiction. He cut his teeth on R.L Stine's Goosebumps series as a child and a fascination with Stephen King's work followed later in life. Jeremy weaves his tales of personal horror from Martinsburg, West Virginia with his cat Lazarus acting as his muse/familiar.

We take our faces for granted, don't we? We look into a mirror, and our face is there. We snap a selfie, and our face grins from the smartphone screen. We run our fingertips across our faces when we wake, and we wash them gently before we sleep. Faces define us. They are portraits of expression, fleshly and familiar, and typically the first thing that people notice in modern society.

We are lost without our faces. We are blank and apathetic drones if we lose that mask of identity. I speak from experience on this matter. It's a topic that's close to my soul.

My name is Jackson Jekyll, and I am faceless. You will find no expression on my face. No smile. No high cheekbones or smooth brow. My poor excuse for a countenance is nothing more than mangled meat, a poorly grafted patchwork of thin skin stretched across the skull that lies beneath. No nose. No lips. Sunken, beady remnants for eyes. A puckered little hole that is supposed to serve as my mouth. Hair nonexistence aside from a few paltry strands like spidersilk across the scalp. I am an aberration — a terrible, unpredictable mistake of a human being.

But I was not always like this. I was handsome once. It seems like a lifetime ago now, but I can still recall the mug that greeted me in the bathroom mirror each morning. Dirty blonde hair, eyes as blue as seawater, and a mouth carved to smirk from ear to ear. Angular features. Cheeks often sporting just the right amount of stubble, and skin unflawed by the ravages of age. I was young, I was pretty, and I was a fool. I thought that face would last for eternity, as perfectly elastic and identifiable as it had always been. But it didn't last. Most pleasing things rarely do.

It was taken from me. Those dashing features stolen in a single moment of doubt and indecision. It was the lead that exited the barrel of a .357 Magnum that obliterated my face, but it was a loathsome beast named Depression that aided me in pulling the trigger. I've always suffered from those bouts of melancholy. Despite my occasional moments of vanity, that shadow serpent depression often managed to slither itself around me, a loving coil to flick a black forked tongue at the sorrow infecting my soul. It weighed me down, and how it whispered, each word devoted to woe.

I found myself lost in the grayest pit of an indifferent world, and I could find no hope to crawl back up to the surface. And so the serpent fed, the serpent teased, and it grew fat as my negative thoughts multiplied. I considered hope a fallacy, and optimism a myth reserved only for the lucky few that fate allowed to experience genuine happiness.

It was an ordinary night full of ordinary stars while ordinary rain pounded on the roof when I decided to eat a bullet. The dreary blackness beyond the window seemed a poetic sign, and I thought if ever I was to blow this miserable brain out of my skull, I couldn't have asked for a more suitable moment in time.

Those memories are lost to me now. It is all fragmented red ruin and a cacophony of sound in my head. My last coherent thought was that I could taste a few brittle specks of skull shrapnel in the back of my throat, and then the lights mercifully cut out.

My life changed forever that night. The person I was changed. The face I once called my own carved down to wrecked ribbons due to my own flighty actions.

I awoke as the pitiful creature that speaks to you now. The surgeons did the best they could with the tools available to them. They crafted a rudimentary ball of meat for me using slices of my inner thighs, my buttocks, and the flab beneath both of my arms. They slathered ointment onto their creation night and day to keep it moisturized, and I sat forlornly in that hospital bed like a fragile human doll. I sucked down my nourishment through a straw and I pleaded with the nurses for a mirror, just an innocent little pocket mirror. My groveling finally paid off and I was reluctantly handed the instrument of torment.

They had to wrestle it from my weak hands to stop the hoarse screams from rattling out of my throat. I was a horror to behold. The skin grafts did nothing but give me something like the pale and twisted features of an unfinished mannequin, a figure that was built so sloppily that God gave up halfway through and tossed me into His great cosmic dumpster.

I was repulsed. I was devastated. I was more lost than ever before. And when a man is locked in sterile purgatory, can you blame him for scrabbling desperately at the first little glimmer of hope that he hears about?

That's what I felt when the new surgeon visited me. His name was Warwick, and he spoke of medical wonders. His hands seemed angelic to me, fingers long and nimble, and he had a habit of patting my poor shoulder after each word of encouragement. He weaved such fanciful dreams in my head, the concept of a meaningful life beyond this terrible mistake that I'd made.

It all came down to two magical words.

Face transplant.

Tissue painstakingly removed from a cadaver and slowly crafted to an entirely new human being. A new face to replace the one I'd lost. A nose, a mouth, and cheeks all my own. The beautiful idea that I'd be granted the gift of living as an actual person again. No more hiding and sulking like a bandaged pariah behind thin plastic curtains.

Warwick even had a recently deceased anonymous donor that had gifted his body to medical science. He said this kindly departed soul would be the perfect face to harvest and plaster across my own feature-less skull. At that moment I could have kissed that selfless corpse. Even the mention of his name filled me up with thoughts of a bright future.

Luther Hyde.

A cadaver making the ultimate sacrifice to ensure that another ruined soul benefits. I only wished I could have gotten to meet Mr. Hyde when he still walked the world. I considered him a saint of the highest order, and I often passed sleepless nights of pain mumbling out prayers to this dearly departed man.

The morning of surgery finally arrived. I gave Warwick my best lip-less smile as the anesthesia took over. He patted my shoulder companionably and told me that he'd see me on the other side and that I'd see myself as an entirely new person. I fell into a slumber both dark and deep, 36 hours of surreal dreams that circled endlessly in my head. All I remember of the dreams is a peeled human face laughing at me, the eyes just ragged bloody holes and the mouth a toothless leer dripping with vile intentions.

I awoke in a drugged stupor, my face as numb as putty, and Warwick's soothing voice drifting down overtop me as I lay there in the hospital's trauma ward. He was telling me about how the procedure was a complete success. He pontificated about the connecting of nerves, blood vessels, and strings of musculature. He told me that I'd be on immunosuppression drugs for an indefinite amount of time to prevent my body from rejecting my new face. All of this washed over me like a jumbled tide, and I simply nodded my slack face at him until he was satisfied that I'd heard all there was to hear.

I flitted in and out of consciousness for those first few days. It was on the 5th day that I awoke vibrant and strong, a sense of unexpected vigor twitching through my limbs. I sat up in bed and demanded a glass of orange juice, and I delighted in the fact that I could feel actual lips struggling to grip the straw and suck down the delicious citrus juice. I tested these new powers carefully at first, and with much more intensity as I became accustomed to their uses. I lifted my cheeks using the muscles beneath. I twitched my brow and wiggled my nose almost imperceptibly. I attempted to grin at one of the prettiest nurses, and I felt something like a heavy grimace settle on my face. She did her best to hide her discomfort, but it didn't bother me at all that she reacted that way. I used to be a man undone, and suddenly I'd been given the chance to build myself back up brick my fleshy brick.

Once more I called for a mirror, and once more my demands were swiftly met. The mirror was placed into my hand so quickly that I got the idea that most of the nurses and orderlies that visited my room were nervous about the idea of crossing me. Perhaps a byproduct of a new face capable of necessary sternness?

The reflection told me the whole story. My informal meeting with Luther Hyde. The face that stared back at me was wholly a stranger. A beetled brow, bulbous nose, and thick, drooping lips. My own eyes sat far back in dark hollows, the eyelids drooping to show redness beneath. The muscles of my new face were still very weak and I could only perform the most basic movements, but the sight alone stirred something within me.

I came to feel a sense of foreboding about this face. Not the superficial ugliness of it, but a feeling that the deeds Mr. Hyde committed in his life were perhaps not so honorable after all. There was a slyness to the countenance; the sort of face that would look at home bundled under a ratty top hat in some stinking Victorian opium den.

I did my best to put these silly thoughts out of my mind. It is a shocking thing to awaken to a reflection that you don't recognize, and I figured it would take time for me to become used to the results of the operation. I vowed to focus on strengthening this face until it suited my purposes, and then finally gaining my freedom beyond the hospital corridors.

And so my journey began anew. I took to the little facial exercises vigorously, all the minute forms of physical therapy meant to help me maximize the potential of this new meat-canvas. Warwick became delighted at the speed of my progress, citing it as a miraculous meshing of dead face to living skull.

Soon my eyebrows danced like caterpillars, my cheeks grew flushed and florid with life, and my thick lips curved up into the most lecherous grin to ever decorate a human mouth. I was the surgical team's star pupil, and how they cooed over their favorite guinea pig.

But for all the speedy physical improvements, there was a battle occurring beneath the surface. It came to me slowly at first, a subtle sense of wrongness on a particularly quiet night. It was a whisper deep in the center of my skull. I know my own thoughts, and this whisper was not born of them. It seemed almost like an internal monologue chanting over and over again, spilling out vague vulgarities and the most repugnant words the English language has to offer.

A sensation would often follow. It is damn near indescribable, but the closest I can come is the feeling of numerous slugs slithering beneath the skin of my face and leaving their sticky slime trails to dry there.

The dreams were the worst. They came in murky fragments, nothing tangible. A street pooled with shadow. The pockmarked faces of urchins and whores lining a gaudy alleyway. The tapping of a cane and the splash of ragged boots in puddles of rainwater. And below these tame images, more gruesome flashes of depravity. Bloody spraying from ape-like knuckles. The thrusting of a pelvis into a malnourished woman, sweat flying and bellows emerging from a barrel chest. Meaty hands caught in the act of strangulation one moment and the self-flagellation the next. A wild twister of disturbing mental pictures and it all seemed to follow that same format.

Whispers in the skull, slug trails beneath the skin, and then the horrid dreams as the grand finale. I thought perhaps the dreams could be a side effect of the anti-rejection medications I was taking, but Warwick assured me that I shouldn't be suffering from any night terrors due to those carefully controlled drugs.

The hospital staff began to notice the changes in me. The nurses acted wary whenever in my presence, and the orderlies that brought my food made certain to keep their hands a safe distance away when delivering my tray. Sometimes I'd catch myself attempting to mumble out suggestive whispers to them, but the muscles beneath were still too disused to produce comprehensible words.

I came to this hospital already in the heart of Hell, but it seems I underestimated how deep the circles of the pit truly are. There was a taste of the infernal to this face that I'd been given. I'd often catch the stench of brimstone in my new nostrils with no ability to account for the origin of the smell. I believe most demons are simply people so twisted and malformed by evil that their humanity strips down to the bone, and the haunting idea that I was wearing such a demon's face would not let me rest.

I felt my face getting stronger and stronger. I was able to chew, swallow, and take down almost all solid foods. I could mimic all the normal emotions: happiness, sadness, fear, anger, etc.

But with each new accomplishment, I felt something like a slip of control from inside of me. Sometimes I felt myself grinning when I had no will to grin. Sometimes my eyes would drift in the sockets and stare at someone I did not want to stare at. A salaciousness was beginning to rule me, and it seemed that I was totally incapable of dialing it back. I began to fear my new face. I began to positively loathe the feel of it against the plain tortured skin underneath. I knew in the innocent depths of what was left of my soul that I must act quickly, and the day my new face spoke for the first time confirmed all my suspicions.

I felt a pull. My vocal cords struggling, my tongue lashing against me, and those wormy lips opening and closing like a fish out of water. Mr. Hyde's face spoke at the hour of midnight, and it addressed me like a subservient dog to be beaten into submission.

"Wanna fuck, Jekyll. Wanna feast and rend and have a bit of fun. I'm melded to your meat, and I'll make a paradise of it. I'll paint it in blood, I'll smear it in shit, and I'll have my fucking fun. The streets call, Jekyll. Soon I'll stroll...and you will surrender this flesh, won't you?"

A gurgling chuckle escaped from the fiend's mouth (my mouth) and the dread that I felt seemed to freeze my limbs beneath the hospital gown. I left Hyde's question unanswered, and soon those chuckles gave way to bubbling snores, little blobs of mucus splattering from the nostrils with each exhaled breath.

I knew what I had to do. My hand closed across the stainless steel surgical shears, and I began to cut with fingers that I still had control over. I slashed and I cut and I hacked, slabs of glistening red meat falling from my new face to stain the pristine hospital sheets. Hyde woke from his slumber, and the sounds he made forced my bladder to let go.

He mewled like a feral tomcat, a carrion eater finally backed into a corner and dying against its will. His lips formed murderous curses, so I cut them off and threw them across the room until they stuck to the wall like plump nightcrawlers. That veiny nose spewed out snot as I stabbed the shears into it, severing carefully constructed cartilage and making a pouring faucet of the flesh lump. I carved into the brow like tough turkey meat, steel scratching against skull as I pierced the thick layer of skin.

After an uncertain amount of time with me cutting and carving and destroying, the act of self-mutilation was finally complete. My face poured with blood and ached like it had been doused in gasoline and set aflame, but I could feel Hyde's influence fading.

His whispers curdled. His sluggish sensations vanished from the skin. The putrid hallucinations of his past revelries went with him, groaning and lamenting towards the death he so rightfully deserved.

Warwick found me shortly after, the surgeon so aghast at my actions that he was forced to grab hold of an EKG machine to keep from toppling over. The star pupil undone. The special guinea pig carved into little more than a gory disappointment.

More skin grafts followed, more moments of sleep, but never another face transplant. I was deemed a failed recipient. I suppose my body did rejection the transplant, but not in the way that the surgeons predicted.

I am faceless again now, just a brittle skull supported by a few tendrils of salvaged skin from the parts of my body that still had it to give. People cringe at the sight of me, but I've never been happier. I am at peace with the remnants of flesh that I now call my own. The world doesn't realize how lucky they are to gaze on this ragged ruin instead of the alternative option.

If they had only seen the face of Hyde.

So much worse. So unapologetically worse...

Param

Susan Snyder

My poem Her Name was selected for the Horror Writers Association Poetry Showcase Volume V. My dark poem The Servant appeared in the Autumn 2017 issue of Illumen. Disturbed Digest published the poem Heartbeat in the June 2018 edition. Reflection, a work of short fiction, can be seen in the #7 issue of Jitter Press. My poem As is My Custom has been published in Jitter Press #7 and will be featured in the relaunch issue of Gallows Hill Magazine in the Spring of 2019. I am a member of the Horror Writers Association.

Sitting in the folding chair in the corner of the room, I lit a smoke with my bloody fingers. I stared at my lover's decimated corpse and took a long drag off the cigarette. I had never met anyone like her, and doubt I ever will again. The encounter was only for one night but more passionate than any of the dozens of women I've picked up at the club.

My eyes grazed over the implements I used over the last few hours. Most were covered in a mixture of blood, skin, lubricant, cum, and hair. They sat on the long metal table along the wall of my basement. Each one was something special and drew a unique response from my lovers. I tried to think outside the box with my instruments. For this last one, I used an immersion blender that I got from my mother last Christmas. I started using it on her breasts but the splatter of tissues and fat was off-putting and killed the mood. I remember walking over to the metal table to wipe my face and noticing that she was still awake. Usually, they'd pass out from the pain. She strained her eyes to me and maintained full eye contact as I walked back over to the cot where she was strapped and bound. She wasn't crying or pleading with her gagged mouth. She looked flushed and intense. My gaze traveled to her quivering legs, and in between them, I saw her orgasm.

Yes, this lover was different. This one let me take her all the way to the end.

I was known at the club for my skills. It wasn't a club exactly but more of a gathering place for like-minded people. There is no alcohol or music, just those of us who want to bring or to feel pain. I rose to the top of the food chain quite quickly- a sadist in a sea of masochists. Drifting only toward the extreme, I have always been selective. There were a few with BIID, the overwhelming desire to become an amputee, and I enjoyed them immensely, but they're rare. I dabbled in severe body modification but there's a lack of passion in those encounters and too much ego.

But this one was different. She stunned me with her ability to stay alert through the pain, to take it in and erupt into pleasure. I made a conscious decision early on to keep her sex intact until the end, to let her have her release.

I continued my reminiscing as I looked over my instruments. The electric knife I used on her wrists and ankles. The pliers for her teeth. The straight razor to slice off her nose, ears, tongue and later, her labia. She moaned and writhed until the very last moment when she couldn't keep those beautiful eyes, always fixed on mine, open any longer.

I took a final drag of my cigarette and put it out in the coffee can filled with ground bones of amputated femurs and humeri I kept under the chair. I loved my little pleasure palace but it was a damp place, smelling of mildew and mold. It was time to return to the warmth of my home upstairs. It was a quiet and isolated farmhouse, many miles from the interference of any neighbors. I would clean up tomorrow. The night's activity and the surprising resilience of my lover tapped all of my energy. I needed to eat and sleep.

I climbed the stairs to the basement door, solid metal and designed to keep sound and lovers alike within. I reached inside my leather apron for the keys. Sharp sickening pain in my gut hit me as soon as one hand grabbed the handle of the door and the other found an empty pocket. Idiot. You fucking idiot! I could see the key on the kitchen table on the other side of the door, clear as day. I had never forgotten that key. Never. Until now.

Phase one: Bloat

I had hoped to clean up my work before the storm arrived. The stone walls of the basement began to seep with water from the downpour outside. That was both a blessing and a curse. I lapped and sucked at the cold damp wall. I was so thirsty from the previous night's excursion, and I never kept any food or water in the basement. That seemed unsanitary and unnecessary. The moisture in the air, however, did not bode well for the decomposition of my lover's corpse. She looked pregnant with the bloat of gas and fluid. Her skin had turned a marbled hue of greenish browns and yellows. My fingertips were shriveled from the dankness and from pressing them against the wet wall when I took a drink.

I spent a long time just thinking. There was not much hope in escaping this situation as I designed that metal door myself. My isolation doomed me. I had no way to communicate with the outside world, and even if I had my cell, there was never a signal down here. Most of my thoughts were just curses at my own stupidity and carelessness. My mind kept seeing that key, mocking me from the safety and warmth of my kitchen table.

Phase two: Fluids

The rain continued. The leaking water in the walls kept my thirst at bay, but my hunger became an insistent and demanding mistress. The smell of the decaying corpse permeated the room. The only relief was a small opening in the bottom corner of the stone foundation where a light breeze could be felt. I walked over there often to cleanse my nostrils of the odor. She was leaking fluids, turning the ivory cot into a tapestry of greens and browns that matched her skin. As revolting as the stench was, my stomach still churned and gurgled with hunger.

I occupied myself with memories of former encounters. Even now, I was consumed with my vice. It was the only identity I knew, and had been since my early twenties, since I found that club. For the first time in a long while, I felt ashamed. Hopeless. Not in control. I threw my head back and screamed. No one would hear me.

Phase three: Maggots

That little opening in the corner of the wall, the one that purged my nostrils of the putrid smell of decay, also allowed insects into the basement. Pacing along the perimeter of the room, some small movement caught my eye. At first, I thought it was more expulsion of gases from her body, creating the illusion of animation. Walking over to her, I leaned in and saw the white squirming larvae, lining her tongue-less mouth. I jumped back instinctively. Then I saw her vaginal cavity leaking squirming maggots. Her mangled breasts had a few as well, still on the surface writhing in the shredded flesh and tissue.

And despite all of this, my stomach growled.

Phase four: Hunger

The small amount of water provided by the continuing rain satiated my thirst and kept me alive. This situation was extreme and hopeless. I am not sure why I didn't use one of those straight razors on my metal table to split open my wrists, to end my suffering. It may have been curiosity, or the sprouting of a small seed of masochism planted by my numerous encounters. This felt to me like an awakening. I wanted to see this through to the end. Just like my lover did. I suppose I owed her that much.

My first taste of her was sitting on the cold floor, flies buzzing about. I had sliced a piece of her torso, from the side below her rib cage. The flesh was a bronze color now, but still somewhat moist and malleable from the dankness. The texture in my mouth felt like wet leather and as my teeth came down on the flesh, juices squeezed from it like the remaining dishwater on an old sponge. My insatiable hunger took over my senses as I went back for more, hacking at her torso with the razor and stuffing her rancid flesh into my mouth. Liquids and the occasional maggot slid down my chin. I didn't care and I didn't stop.

Phase five: The End

I vomited almost continuously throughout the next few hours. The pain of the abdominal cramping became almost too much to bear. I stayed curled up on my side, holding myself on the cold concrete floor, for a long time. I stared at the pile of vomit, the macerated remains of my binge.

I walked over to my lover and kissed her hard lips. She had taken me all the way to the end, as I did her. I had met my match. Even if I was to escape my dungeon, what sexual encounter would ever light a candle to this? I had reached the edge, the param, the highest limit of enlightenment.

Now I finally hold that straight razor with another purpose. A final purpose. I truly hope I will see her there, on the other side. Perhaps we can do this again.

The Fishwife

Jeannie Warner

J eannie Warner spent her formative years in Colorado, Canada, and California, and is not afraid to abandon even the most luxurious domestic environs for an opportunity to travel almost anywhere. She has a useless degree in musicology, a checkered career in computer security, and aspirations of world domination. She has short stories published in YA anthologies, weird science magazines, a movie credit, and lives for podcasts.

"Cast off the bowline, ya odious harpy!"

She was already unwinding the thick rope as he yelled, and with a well-practiced heave tossed it the short distance across the water to the prow. "Done. Don't come back this time. Jump overboard after a mermaid and follow her home."

"She'd be more welcoming than you, ya cold fish."

"Fish smell better than you. I'd rather bed a willing eel."

It was a routine parting, as it had been for the last twenty-odd years of marriage, with very little variation save for the general synonyms and invective. Some people can tell you to the day and hour when they got married, as they celebrate their anniversary and other romantic occasions. For Mel, after the first decade, she would have hazarded that it had been in the fall because of the rain and the dead, wet leaves that swept along the ground and stuck to everything. She didn't want to think about it.

She did remember a blond and smiling boy with twinkling blue eyes who asked her to dance, and a lot of ale afterward. Then there was a tavern room upstairs, and some crisp cotton sheets, and a lot of sweating and grunting that eventually ended up with the two of them hastily standing in front of a priest after breakfast the next day. She'd been secretly proud to marry a Waterman with his own boat, a thirty-footer with bright red sails.

Having secured a wife in that whirlwind courtship that had too much to do with racing and regattas, dancing in the streets, two kegs of ale and a bet, Miles Waterman was content and kind enough in the first three years of wedded bliss on the shores of Rhode Island until their union proved barren. Miles had planned sons to leave his fishing business to, and when it became apparent that no sons (or even daughters) were going to be forthcoming between him and the local judge's daughter he was angry. When he started shortening Melanie to Mel, she, in turn, took to calling him Mac as the sharper sound went better with his new disposition.

But Mac was an upright man, a pillar of the scattered rural coastline community, and Mel was a good daughter of her family. Mac always said he'd never raise a hand to his woman, not like some. It was the subtler manifestations of his anger that turned Mel bitter as she navigated a constant stream of verbal cuts and belittlement that only slowly lost their ability to draw blood. She'd prayed for children both for herself and to sweeten Mac's temper.

When children didn't come, Mel gave up on miracles. Life was full enough, a constant struggle against the elements and each other, and the business-like partnership endured as the lines grew deeper in both faces.

Mel turned her back on the boat as it headed away from their dock and out into the bay proper, and climbed the shale steps up to the small fish shop with a cottage attached to the back. Her step was a little lighter going up than it was coming down in anticipation of having the usual two days of quiet and solitude. Out on the water, Mac was already chugging out past the promontory that guarded their tiny inlet into the deeper waters of the bay and the sea beyond.

There were dark grey clouds growing tall on the horizon, and Mel's lips curved into a smile that may have been a touch mean. "Oh look. A storm. Hope you get sick and lose your lunch all over yourself." It never ceased to darkly amuse her that, of the two of them, she was the one immune to seasickness while Mac was the one who manned the boat and kept their little shop supplied with fish. Some seasons there was more profit to be made in shellfish, but Mac's usual routine was to head further out and troll for larger game.

With a storm coming there was a great deal of work to do, and Mel fell to it with the usual surge of energy that came from being alone. She hummed to herself as she stacked up and secured the drying racks, roping together the empty wooden trays so that later she could drag them all down together to scrub them in the sea. The pots and pound nets were already secured, but she gave the ropes a tug in passing just to be certain. The wind picked up, tugging at her hair as she finished the work outside the shop. A circle around the outside secured all the shutters against the wind. Her hands were nigh as rough and weatherworn as Mac's were, and she felt a weather-wise ache in the knuckles as she rubbed them against her hips and headed indoors.

Unexpectedly, the squall turned into a tempest and shrieked like an injured cat to rattle the whole building with wind. The wind ripped shingles off the roof until Mel was certain the whole thing would blow off. She hid under the covers and shivered. A distant crash sounded, warning her that the hoist down at the dock for the nets had broken, and other damage seemed inevitable. A solitary boat on the water dwelled in her thoughts more than she had expected, but not with fondness or worry; more a concern for how she would make her way without the small income that dried fish provided for winter.

The storm continued the next two days, though the ferocity broke first and hardest against the shore with the leading edge of the front, and by the second day, it was merely a hard, steady rain backed by winds that blew it sideways. On the third day, the sun rose again. Mel unlocked the shutters from the windows, then headed out to start putting their domain back to right as best she could.

A short trip into the village for a fresh bake and news was numbing for her at first. Seven boats lost, they said, the women gathered around with their overcoats pulled tight and scarves tied firmly under their chins. Seven families torn asunder, but there was very little weeping and wailing. You knew the possible cost if you plied the bay and sea beyond. The dark waters claimed a few from each generation. This harvest was more violent than any in recent years, but at the pub, there were dire stories of how many had been lost forty years and more. Still, Mel found a few touches on the shoulder from the townsfolk, and the baker charged her half the usual rate for bread and flour.

Mel searched the horizon where sea touched that night for a familiar ship, but there was nothing incoming with the tide. After a couple of days, she stopped looking up and shading her eyes to check. She also stopped wearing a scarf over her hair while at home, letting the wind off the sea rake her hair into a wild tangle that she spent an hour each night brushing out before bed. She took stock of the salt fish that remained and set up the closed sign in the shop window. The drying racks she wrestled down to clean as she had intended days ago, but instead of re-stacking them behind the back she dragged the lot out to the road with a new sign offering them up for sale. Inquire within.

The next day Mel twisted her long brown hair up into a bun, put on her scarf, and walked the five miles down the road to church. There the hum of gossip was still all about the storm, and what had broken, and who needed to rebuild. Mel was quiet with her eyes down on the cover of her prayer beads, not yet ready to mention Mac's loss at the service to endure the full sympathy or, worse than that, congratulations anyone who knew Mac well.

But she did mention to two women who kept sheep that if they needed help with their shearing or carding, that she was thinking of working more outside the home with the fish running lighter the last year. Both women clucked their tongues, exchanged glances, and assured her that Mel should come by and pick up some baskets of the raw wool. She thanked them both humbly, mild and quiet as she had learned to be over the years. Mel followed the women and brought baskets of newly-shorn wool home with her.

Back home she kicked off her shoes to go barefoot, then washed and carded the wool overnight by touch after blowing out the lantern to save oil. She stroked the fibers and eased the teeth of the combs through the thick curls as carefully as she did her own hair. In the morning she took the smooth rovings back to the ladies that had offered the opportunity as charity, and they paid her with tones of surprise at her quickness and offered more baskets to work on.

Mel started to sing as she worked. She found that she still fit an old holiday dress from her younger days and took it out of its papers and lavender to wear it again, and in a few days her calves and feet were almost tan again. The lanolin from working the wool softened her hands.

Outside, as if abashed at its own violence, the sea and sky turned fair and seemed determined to stay that way.

The next seven-day eve she put on shoes and attended church. Besides the wool, Mel found net mending and darning to do for others in the parish. She shaped clay and the local rocks into simple planters and went calling to beg a single bag of earth or compost humbly from each of the other houses to fill them, along with bits of seed. She put rocks in the oven as she baked, or by the stove, and lined her little garden with them as night fell so the extra bit of warmth would help the seeds germinate into little bits of growth that she sang to and covered with sailcloth when the wind blew too harshly.

Mel didn't sleep the deep sleep of the exhausted any longer. She searched inside herself to find a word, an idea for what kept her moving and thinking and dreaming and discovered that the only one that fit what she felt was contentment. The next evening when the rain was falling and the wind tossing the waves, a knock sounded at the door. Mel was awake to answer it and open wide the door with a smile on her lips.

The smile faded. Mac stood there, wet head to toe and smelling of the sea and of rotting sea things. He didn't move at first, standing stock still on the doorway as Mel's mouth opened and closed like a fish. The lightness in her chest from the last few weeks plummeted, and she felt the weight of stones sinking on her lungs and stomach, filling her body with stones. She'd almost forgotten what it felt like to be made of stone.

"I live here, aye?" Mac's voice was soft, almost a whisper.

"Yes." Her fingers gripped the door frame hard, going white-knuckled. She ought to let him in, but she was frozen in place.

"May I enter?" Outside the sea was hushed, the waves barely seeming to lap at the shore.

Mel couldn't remember the last time her husband had used the word 'may' when it wasn't in a conversation about the month that came after April. The surprise of it loosened her fingers, and she nodded and stepped back to let him in. Water dripped and fell into little puddles about his feet as he stepped through the door. She closed it after him and turned to look him over.

Mac stood staring, looking around slowly like a man on a reprieve from the gallows, given one final chance to see the world. His pale blue eyes seemed even paler than usual, as if the storm and ordeal had leached the color from them. His face, too, the weather-worn tan sallow as though he had lain ill for the weeks of being gone, and he stood with his clothing all in rags. It was the smell of the latter that prompted Mel to speak up in her more normal brisk tone. "You've brought in all the dead fish in the world with you, Mac. Strip out of it all, and I'll get it off in the wash."

He turned slowly to look at her. "I'm sorry. Yes, of course." And with the pale eyes on her face, right there by the door Mac stripped off every inch of his wet clothing and bundled it up in his arms. "Where do you want me to put it?"

Mel furrowed her brow. Mac was normally a notorious prude about skin. Back when they had made love, it had always been in the full dark. "Did you hit your head or something?" And because he looked almost vulnerable for the first time in memory, she stepped up to touch at his forehead, then a hand over his skull in search of the goose egg that must surely be there.

He flinched very slightly at the touch of her fingers before going still to let her feel along his skin as she pleased. "How long...was I gone?"

"Been nearly two months since the storm." Mel took the clothes from him and went to deposit them with her other washing, to determine in better light what could be salvaged. "I thought you were gone."

She took a breath in anticipation of a fight. "I sold the racks. Didn't think you were coming back."

Naked he stood and watched her move about the small house. He made no move to cover himself, nor do more than watch her with a wariness that echoed her own uncertainty. "I didn't think I was, either."

She found it was difficult, after the habits of so many years, to simply look at all that nakedness. Her eyes drifted around the small one-room house they shared. "We can try to buy them back, I suppose, if we can get a note of credit or something. I already spent the money on other necessities."

"We can sell fresh fish instead."

"You saved the ship?" It was a note of hope in Mel's sea of stomach-churning unease.

Mac paused as if considering the nature of her question, then nodded. "Yes. It will be down at the water tomorrow morning."

Mel smiled at him at that, and her tone warmed at the thought of avoiding more debt. "Oh, that's very good news." She wanted to ask more, ask what happened and where he'd been. But this fragile moment of not fighting seemed too precious to waste on bad stories that might upset him. She didn't want Mac to snap back into his old self, their old way of arguing. "Do you want some tea then?"

"Some tea? Yes." Mac nodded, and then he smiled back at her.

She'd never seen this particular expression on the older Mac, and she had no reaction she knew to be appropriate for that arrangement of whiskers and wrinkles and teeth. It stole the breath from her lungs and the strength from her joints. Mel sat down abruptly in a chair and buried her face in her hands. Her shoulders shook from not-quite crying - something more like shudders from gulping down too many thoughts and emotions at once. Her eyes were dry as she sobbed and rocked.

Mac knelt down before her, laying his hands over hers. "Don't cry. Please don't cry. Have I upset you? I do not need tea if it makes you sad."

It was too much, this unexpected softness. Mel had always been proud of being strong, with a kind of desperate stubbornness that comes of constant opposition. The tears started flowing then, and Mac gathered her into his arms. With a strength born of lifting heavy nets from the sea, he lifted and carried her off to the corner behind a curtain where their bed lay and set her lightly down in it. For a while, he simply held her and stroked her hair in silence, and this set it all off again in a new bout.

But you can only cry for so long, and after gulping for air and learning to breathe again, Mel's whole body started to relax. He'd grown better at silence, and she found his hand on her hair pleasant. At last, she turned in his arms, reddened eyes staring into a face shadowed with the candlelight behind. "I must look a sight," she croaked, sniffling and pushing back a tangled lock behind one ear.

"You look beautiful to me," Mac offered solemnly, and kissed her. His lips curved, and he licked her lips again lightly. "And right now, you taste of the sea."

"So do you," Mel whispered, because he did. And because she didn't know what else to do in this impossible evening, she opened her arms and lips.

He made love to her like it was the first time, and her body was new and young again. In truth, it was the first time Mel could actually consider the term making love for what they were doing. She'd always thought the words something off-kilter to reality, which was more like plowing or fucking. The terms of the working fields and land seemed more appropriate to what happened in the marriage bed. But this was lovemaking, all strange and new, and she recognized it for what it was and found that she was not so far gone in indifference to crave it.

Afterward, when they were laying together entangled on the tatters of their marriage quilt, Mel cried again. But this time her tears were hot and slow and crept out of the corner of her eye to dampen his chest. When they, too, dried up, she drifted off to sleep with the notion that she could get used to him smelling like fish.

When she woke up, she was alone in bed. The naked Mac was looking over the first pages of their Bible, touching the names on the family tree. When he realized her eyes were open, he closed it with care and put it back on the shelf. "I'll need to go fish today, Melanie. I fear I've shown up on your doorstep with nothing in my hands."

Her breath caught, steadied. It was a name he'd not used in a decade or more. "Are you sure you don't need your rest?" Not that he'd seemed injured last night. She was sore, but it was not unpleasant.

"Our family needs to eat. I'll be back tomorrow."

She rose and picked out clothing for him from the places she'd packed it away. "Alright then. Take care." The words felt foreign in her mouth, but right to say. This Mac she wanted to take care, just in case another bump on his head set him back the way he was. The way he had been, the way that they had been together, that was a slow and tedious death.

His smile at her was blinding as if the night's practice had taught him how to do such a thing in the proper way. "Aye," he said. "Be well, my Melanie."

When he was just out of sight down the slope, she ran after him barefoot on the pebbles to watch him walking to the water. There lodged on the shore by the wreck of the dock was his boat, looking worse for the wear in a storm. The windows were shattered in the wheelhouse, the lines snapped off in places and dangling from the bow and sides. Mel sat down hard, staring at the ship. Mac boarded it, hopping lightly from broken spars from the dock that stuck up at odd angles. The ship moved under his hands out into the waves like a hound for its master, bounding from wave to wave as Mac headed out into a foggy bay.

She sat there all day and all night, no hunger in her for the way her stomach was tied up in knots of dread and anticipation. "Surely that was a ghost," she whispered but found no prayers appropriate in her thoughts at the idea. He'd seemed all too solid, and the seagulls crying in his absence were like the sounds she'd made last night, sounds she couldn't recall making before. By late afternoon, Mel was sure he'd never come again; that one night was all she'd have in a kind of atonement for her years of misery.

But there came the boat again at evening tide, riding low in the water for the hold full of fish in greater abundance than she could ever remember. She stood up and waved, even before he might see her and wave back. As he got closer Mel ran down the hill and splashed into the water, helping to take a line to secure onto one of the few upright pieces of timber.

Mac laughed an open and joyful sound, and pulled her out of the water into his arms to kiss her soundly. "Did you think I wouldn't be back, wife?"

"I hoped you would," she whispered, wildly surprised to discover it was true. Together they finished tying up the boat and unloaded the ship. With the cargo of fish safely stowed, they held hands and ran to the cabin where they fell into bed as clothing went everywhere.

The next day she took the cart into town in three loads, selling his catch to each shop and wholesale market that supplied the bigger cities along the bay. And then the next day after that, for it seemed that fish were eluding the nets of the other fishermen. She sold everything Mac caught, the bounty a welcome sight in the village.

The following seven-day eve as she readied to go to church, Mel found herself queasy. Rushing for the bathroom, she was noisily and unexpectedly sick into it as Mac held her hair. Miles, rather. She had started to think of his name as Miles more often than just Mac. "I fear

I'm ill," she offered wanly, wiping at her mouth as he'd tenderly (and helpfully) held her hair, which she had started to put up neatly once more.

His eyes lit up, and he reached for her belly. "You're pregnant already? This is splendid."

Pain pierced her heart, and she pulled away from his touch. "Impossible. We know that's not true. It's likely just a touch of ague."

"Of course, it is true," he followed her, slipping his arms around her. "You're going to be a mother, and our children will be strong and brave."

Her laughter was very like a sob. "That is the worst lie you've ever told me, Miles Waterman. Haven't we fought and hated each other for these many years because of the truth? That I'm barren and you never forgave me for it?"

He turned her until her cheek pressed against his, one hand stroking her hair. "Shh. Melanie, I tell you true that you are a mother, beautiful and strong and stubborn enough to bring my babies into this world." Miles was silent for a moment, then sighed. "I had not thought I could love you so."

Mel could not help her heart melting. "It'd be a miracle if it was even one, let alone twins."

The kiss in her hair was light. "Babies. Trust me, wife. I will keep you safe and warm and well until they breathe, and cry with you at the new life we've made."

Her arms crept around him in turn. "I wanted children. I used to pray, you know."

"Aye." And with that, they held each other for another long moment before parting to go tend to their separate tasks. Mel didn't go to church that day, finding more than enough to do about their small house to make room for children as Miles went off to sea. She kept up with the carding but found more energy to earn that little bit of extra income with the thought of bounty for children to come.

Two weeks passed, and she found her dress tighter across the middle. Alone in their rooms, Mel stripped off her dress and stood in nothing but her hair as she felt the rounding of her belly under her hands. There was a faint flutter, a sign of life that had her crying once more. She counted the weeks and reckoned what she'd known of pregnancy and childbirth from her youth and of the other women in the village.

Mel was no fool. This was too fast, too sudden, and she was no angel to be expecting a miracle. She also knew there was a woman in Newport that was murmured to take care of unwanted children when they came too often, or to a maid not yet married. All the women knew of her.

Mel took a deep breath, knowing that she'd not be taking the water ferry over to visit her. She had wanted children too long. Any children.

That night when Miles held her, Mel turned in his embrace so that her back rested warm against his chest. He always smelled of fish. She inhaled deeply, and drew his arms about her, feeling her skin so much warmer than his. "Tell me something, Miles?"

"Anything, sweet."

"Will our babies be...human?"

He went still against her for a long moment, and she couldn't feel him breathing. His arms tightened to pull her closer. "Will it matter so much?"

Melanie considered it gravely. She thought of the church, and of what is proper, and of the shadowed half-life she'd known before Miles showed up on her doorstep. She shook her head slowly. "I'll love them all the same." Her words came slowly, feeling for the truth in they might carry. "Will I survive?"

Miles sighed and laid a kiss on the crown of her hair. "I fear all they'll get to know of their mother is the stories I'll tell them."

Tears brimmed, but Mel took a deep breath and twisted around to face him, looking deep into his eyes. There were depths of emotion there, of boundless warmth and the cold of the deep where dark things lie. Her fingers traced his cheek. "Mac died, didn't he?"

His expression grew more guarded, but he nodded. "Aye."

"And you're not a spirit, come to comfort me?"

His teeth flashed white in the gloom as he grinned. "Spirits do this?" And he pushed her back into the mattress to prove how very earthly he was, even with his sweat tasting of the sea. When they were both wrung out, he stayed on top of her and rested on his elbows. Miles traced her brow and nose with a fingertip. "I'm from the Deep, but I love your eyes. I love your hair, the color of earth but with growing things. I loved you from the moment I saw you. You will know no pain in childbirth, I promise you absolutely."

Mel's chose only to hear the first words. "You love me?"

"Do you doubt it?"

Her hand found his, fingers interlacing. "No." She kissed him once more and pulled him down to rest against her fully. In her belly, she felt the swimming of small, live things as it pressed between them. "Will our babies live in the sea or on land?"

"We will stay here for a few days. I'll take them into the sea after. They will know what it is to be human before I teach them their true forms. They'll honor their mother all their lives," he promised, kissing her brow. "And I will love you forever, until the world is all made of ocean and our people – our children - return from the depths to their rightful place overall."

"I reckon that's more than I ever hoped for," Mel whispered and closed her eyes.

The Hollers

C. C. Rossi

C. C. Rossi is an author working in the medical field in the urban wilds of Detroit with his 2 Kuvasz. He has been published in multiple magazines and anthologies, and is currently at work on his third novel, a love story about murder, body modification, and ancient German black magic.

Granny had the hollers again last nite, screaming like she was bein' torn apart by wild animals. Pa told me to just ignore her, but it's gettin' hard to sleep with all that noise. I mentioned it to Honey-gurl when she came over this morning to tend to Momma's boils, cause I knew that she was sorta sweet on me and that Pa is sweet on her. I figured that maybe she would put the thought into Pa to do sumthing about the hollers. Its gettin' reel hard for me to work our fields, do my work for the Bullough's, and then cum home to write in my diary without no sleep. Course, I guess it could be a lot worse—-we all could have the hollers.

BOY OH BOY THINGS ARE shure getting strange around here. If it weren't for Momma needing me around to help with everything, I'd head off for the Dakotas at next sun-up. I heard frum Honey-gurl they still have clean water up out there, and don't have to worry about boars eattin all their crops and killing and eattin little babies, what few are left. But I can't leave Momma, not at least until she gets better.

I need to start focusin' on the main points if I want to sharpen my writing skills so that when I get to the Dakotas I can be a writer and not stay a farm worker. Two nights ago, after Honey-gurl was over, Granny started in on her hollerin' again jus as me and Pa and Momma finished dinner. Momma got up to wash the dishes, but usually Pa won't let her because her sores—which are gettin' worse, especially on her arms and hands, lookin' like little pieces of rotten green cauliflower — open in the wash water and the dishes come out brown and smellin' real bad. But this time he jus sat back in his chair and gave me mean sideways glances.

Momma finally finished the dishes and then waddled down to the basement to sleep. Down there you could close the big storm doors and not hear Granny screaming so loud. Pa watched Momma, and when he was shure she was all the way down the stairs, he limped into the smokin' den and called me in with him. I sat down on the hard wooden floor while Pa sat in his favorite rocking chair, got out his big pipe and stuffed it full of dreamy-weed. I don't like dreamy-weed much cause it makes me feel like I'm floating around and dreamin' even though I'm awake, but I took a few puffs anyway cuz Pa always offers and says it's rude not to take somethin' that's offered to you.

We sat for a while and my head started gettin' all funny-feeling like it was floating off my shoulders. I put my hands on top of it to stop it from floatin' away and Pa started laughing, showing off his mouthful of green, decaying teeth, and even though I wasn't happy I started laughin' too. We sat and laughed until I thought I was gonna puke. Pa did puke but he didn't care, just sat on the chair and played with the green chunky puddle on the floor with his bare feet until we both got quiet.

"Not a real preety sight is it, a grown old man playin' with his own juices," he finally said. I shrugged my shoulders and stayed quiet.

"I used be a strong young buck, sure as hell stronger then you," he continued on, his voice shaky but defiant, "but that was a long time ago, back when me and your ma were jus startin' together, thinkin' maybe we could leave here and make something' better for ourselves then our Ma and Pa...thinkin that maybe we all was over the time of the hollers."

He grew quiet again and I tried to get the thick fog out of my head frum the dreamy-weed, when Granny started her screams. Me and Pa both jumped, and then he started giggling. But it wasn't a happy sort of giggle, it was one like when yer real nervous and it made me nervous to hear him do it. I tried to get up and leave but his eyes got real wide and he stood up real fast.

"Did I say you could leave, boy?" he growled. I shook my head and quickly sat back down.

"I know what you're thinkin', that maybe your Pa is gettin' weak in the head, that maybe he's cracking jus like this ol' crazy world," he said, his scarecrow-thin figure towering over me, a line of dark, swollen boils snakin' from his chin down his neck. "Well, maybe I am and maybe I ain't, but it doesn't matter, cause, sumtimes a man jus can takes so much and then he can't take no more." He stopped, and then did sumthing I never thought I'd see my Pa do. He broke down and cried. Four what seemed like forever he cried like a little child and that made me even more nervous then his giggling.

"I'm okay," he blubbered after a couple more minutes, his eyes all red and puffy. "It's not an easy thing, this here life. Watching your Ma fall apart, not havin' a wife to couple with when the urge comes over me." He stopped for a second and looked at me hard. "You been gettin' those urges yet, boy?"

I thought of Huney-gurl and how good it felt to have her lick my pecker-head and put it in her mouth, even with all the nasty boils she had coverin' her tongue, and I was thinkin' how I would do jus about anything to have her do it again. But then I remembered how I caught Pa and her in Granny's bedroom one day when they was supposed to be changin' her beddin', but instead Honey girl was sittin' at the head of the bed, combing what was left of Granny's hair in one hand and pulling mightily on Pa's pecker with the other until he spilled his thin, watery seed all over the floor. I didn't think they seen me peekin', but Pa always looked at me funny from that day on.

"No, sir," I said, keepin' my eyes down so he couldn't see the lie in them. "I ain't been havin' those urges."

"You will soon enough," he said, more quiet like now that he had quit crying. "Soon enough to make you realize why God brought all the bad that he did on us, soon enough to make you realize that sumtimes, a man has to do things that eats up his soul." Suddenly, like she was agreein' with him, Granny let out another powerful scream, enough to shake the foundations of the house.

"I can't fuckin stand it!" Pa yelled, real loud and angry like while shaking his fist at the dirty ceiling. "What more do you want, you fuck-er? Didn't we sacrifice enough for you? Didn't enough blood spill for you? What the fuck more do you want?"

He broke down and started crying again, and I didn't know if he was yellin' at Granny or God. I hoped it was Granny, cause we sure didn't need any more wrath of God coming down on us. When I got up again to leave, Pa just stood there and didn't say anything, so I went into the my corner room and wrapped myself up tight in my blankets, hoping I could drown out Pa's sobbing and Granny's hollerin' and maybe get some sleep.

I SHURE HOPE I CAN remember all that has happened today, cuz when I finally get to the Dakotas I know these here writings will make me a lot of money, if people know the whole story. I shoulda known that sum mighty weird things wood be happening as soon as I opened my eyes and seen some brite sunlight beamin' through the cracks in the ceiling. Seein as how Pa always gets me up at least an hour before sunrise I knew sumthin' was up, and it wasn't long before I realized something else was different: Granny wasn't hollerin' anymore.

Now I knew that meant one of two things, that either Granny had died or she had gone somewhere, and that if she had gone somewhere it meant somebody had took her. It had been weeks since she had been able to walk, her legs puffed up like thick tree logs and covered in sores that leaked red and black goo that smelled like someone's dirty asshole. This made me feel bad, since I could remember how Granny was nice to me when I was smaller and would give me food from her plate even though she was skinnier then me back then. And I was damn skinny.

I looked for Pa but he wasn't around, so I went up the stairs, and halfway up noticed Grannie's door was open. I knew that she wouldn't be up there but I had to look anyway, so I went the rest of the way up and shure enough, no Granny, just some piles of soiled clothes on the floor along with some dark, putrid-smelling puddles of stuff I had never seen and didn't want to see or smell again. I left the room and closed the door so the nasty stink wouldn't cum downstairs and then went back down myself. I figured that maybe Ma wud know where Granny had gone cuz I had already figured that it was probably Pa who had took her somewhere.

I usually don't go down in the basement. Ma doesn't holler like Grannie but she's got a whole bunch of sores the size of ripe grapes all over her body that pop in bright sunlight, so Pa boarded up all the windows to make it dark down there, even in the day. I lit a candle-wax lantern, then walked real slow and careful down the stairs and stood at the bottom for a couple minutes to let my eyes adjust to what little light there was.

Ma was in bed and not moving at all, and I thought that maybe she was dying or even maybe dead, but then she let out a loud wet fart and I was happy cause that meant she was still alive. I was gonna go over and try and wake her up to find out where Pa and Granny were when I felt a hand go under my legs and grab my balls. I damn near soiled my pants and screamed even though I didn't want to. Ma jus turned over and kept on sleeping. I jumped back to the foot of the stairs and put up my fists even though at first I thought it was a devil come to take Ma away and would get me instead.

"Did I scare ya?" Honey-gurl giggled, holding her hand over her mouth, her eyes buggin' out even more then usual.

"What the hell are you doin down here?" I said, my voice cracking and full of scared.

She stepped closer. "I'm here to take care of your Momma." Even though she wasn't very pretty with her long nose, thick black eyebrows and big yellow teeth like a rabbit, I didn't really mind her gettin' closer cuz then I could see her titties better and the way her pert nipples poked out frum underneath her shirt.

"Maybe I should be the one askin' what you're doin' down here," she said, putting her hands on her skinny hips.

"I live here and I'm entitled to go where I please," I said, a little more loud since my heart didn't feel like it was gonna jump out of my chest anymore.

She moved even closer to me and started rubbin' her hands up and down my chest. "I was thinkin' maybe you knew I was down here and wanted to do some playin'. Is that what you were thinking?"

I really hadn't been thinkin' that at first, but when she was that close and rubbin' on me I really couldn't think of anything else with my pecker damn near busting out of my pants. I grabbed her shoulders but she pulled away and walked over to Ma's bed. Giggling, she took off her pants and even in the dark I could see a patch of dark curly hair between her legs and I was damn near half crazy as she began to rub herself right there next to Ma.

"What's the matter?" she said. "Don't you want to learn how to do me like your Pa does me?"

By that point I was gettin' wild, half of me wanting to do whatever she wanted, and the other half full of fear that Ma would wake up and see us.

"Why don't we go upstairs?" I said. "We can go up there and I can lock all the doors."

"I don't wanna go upstairs," she said real loud, and I was afraid that Ma would wake up but I was gettin' crazy watching Honey-gurl work on herself. I didn't know what to do.

"C'mon," Honey-gurl said, "you come over here and after you do me I'll do you."

As stupid as I knew it was, I was ready to get down on my knees and start lickin' on her honey-pie even though it smelled like a big pile of dead carp, but then I heard the upstairs door open and realized that Pa was home. I stood there like a stone, scared and crazy as Pa started to bellow for me. Honey-gurl didn't do a thing except continue rubbing herself and let out little moans now and then. It was only when I heard

Pa's footsteps on the top stairs that I made myself move, and the only place I could figure ongoing was underneath Momma's bed.

I guess one day I might rite a whole lot more on how I felt that afternoon, laying in the dust and mold underneath Momma's bed. How it was that Pa came down to see Honey-gurl gettin' herself all wet and excited, and how he started lickin' on her like a thursty pig lappin' up water, all the while standing next to the bed with Momma snoring away. How, after Honey-gurl had licked Pa's little pecker up and down, the open sores on her tongue leaving a trail of stringy blood and pus, she tugged on it real fast until Pa gave a mightly grunt and dribbled out a weak stream of man-juice onto her chin and chest. When Pa was finally finished, they both started gigglin' like two naughty kids and walked upstairs, holding hands.

I don't know how long I layed under the bed, but I knew it was a long time. My pecker and balls hurt from stayin' hard so long watching Pa and Honey-Gurl, I was sick to my stomach from the sharp smells of dead fish and pus and cum, and I guess all of that made me pissed off enough so that I went right up them stairs and into the living room, not caring if Pa and Honey-gurl was there or not.

Pa was up there all right, sleeping on the floor buck naked, a half-filled pipe of dreamy-weed next to him. Honey-gurl was nowhere to be seen, which was probably good cause I don't know if I could have held back my hate if I wood have seen them couplin'. At first I didn't even try to wake him, but then I just went and kicked him hard in the ribs, busting open a sore the size of a ripe tomato, spraying dark brown fluid everywhere.

"Where's Granny?" I asked, feeling tingly and hot as he looked up at me with bloodshot eyes. I knew he knew that it really wasn't all my worry about Granny that made me kick him but my hate from havin' watched him and Honey-gurl.

"No, boy," he said, shaking his head slow frum side to side. I kicked him again harder, and I felt good and bad at the same time, almost like when Honey-gurl kissed and sucked my pecker-head.

Pa didn't even try to get up and fight me. He jus lay there with a look in his eyes that scared me and gave me strength at the same time. "All right," he finally said, his voice raspy and cold, "I'll tell ya all the things," and suddenly I didn't want to hear any of it. I jus wanted to run out of the house, but I knew I hada stay cause it was my time to know.

"It's kinda funny, you and me talkin' here," Pa started out, "jus like me and my Pa talking a long time ago. Course, I was younger then you and had more respect for the commandments and didn't go and kick the shit out of him." He stopped for a minute, maybe waiting for me to apologize or something, but when he seen I wasn't, he kept on talking.

"I never told you this before, boy, but my Pa, your Grandaddy, was there when it first all came down on us. He was just a youngin, but he remembered it all, back when men still could fly through the sky in air machines. He told me sumtimes he thought that's maybe why God sent the sickness down, cause man was gettin' too close to God's own house. I used to think about those words and spent many a hour on my knees prayin' about it. But I don't do that anymore, cause I think God is jus watchin' us now to see if we learned our lesson, and now and then he still sends the hollers down to remind us it could all come back, every terrible bit of it."

"Back in your Grandad's day it was a million times worse, cause back then there was a million times more people, and damn near most of 'em with the hollers. We've always been country folk, and your granddaddy thought that by bein' in the country the hollers wouldn't get to us. But he was wrong." Pa pushed himself into a sittin' position, grabbed his pipe, tried to light it, then gave up as he continued with his story.

"Maybe all that remembering don't mean a thing. Most all of the people are dead and we live like the old times and that's that. Cept of course when it comes back into your own home like it has to us, like to your Granny and I don't know—" He stopped suddenly and coughed, and I could see spots of blood in his yellow spit. When he was finally done he looked up at me hard. "So you really wanna go see what anger God still has in him? All right then, boy," he said, his eyes never changin' their hard stare, "go see her. Go see her and see what God does to show us who's the real boss."

Pa finally quit talkin' then and stood up real slow, holding his side where I kicked him. He walked over to the old cabinet that stood in the other corner of the house and pulled an old brown piece of paper out of the bottom drawer.

"This here's a map of the Bullough's land," he said, handin' me the paper. "The red circle in the corner of the wheat field is where there are three old oak trees, probably older then the time of the hollers. The middle tree of them is the one where your Granny is."

I took the map from him and looked it over. Although I had never been anywhere far away from the house, I reckoned I could figure out where the tree was without too much problem.

"Hey, boy," I heard my Pa say. I looked up and damned if he hadn't come up with the tree-splittin' axe in his hands, and I figured that he was gonna pay me back for kickin' him, but he just handed it to me nice and easy.

"Boars might be out," he said quietly. "No need for you to give 'em an easy meal."

"Thanks, Pa," I said, and I wanted to say more, and part of me even wanted me to say that I loved him, but as soon as he gave me the axe he turned around an finally lit up his pipe, and so I headed on out the door, prayin' that I wasn't gonna make an easy meal for the boars.

The sun had already gone under the horizon as I crossed our last field of rye and moved onto the Bulloughs land. Pa told me once that the Bullough family had kept this land for six generations. During the time of the hollers they had even formed their own army to keep the land, spilling a lot of blood so it could be theirs forever. This made me feel kinda funny, thinkin' that maybe I was walkin' on somebodies blood or maybe even their bones, but I tried to put it out of my mind as I kept on movin'.

I'm not proud to say it, but I was gettin' scared bout then, and even having second thoughts about what I was doin'. The winds had picked up so that they was blowing hard and makin' all sorts of funny noises, and when I had crossed our creek I had found a pretty fresh pile of boar shit on the banks. It was gettin' dark fast, with storm clouds hiding any sign of the moon or stars. Now, I don't think that I'm a coward, but as I was cresting the next hill I was jus about ready to turn around, so I dropped to my knees and started praying for strength like I used too when I was a child, and all of a sudden the sky got lit up as bright as daylight by a lightning bolt bigger then I had even saw before.

I think it was a sign frum God, cuz right after that lightning bolt I heard it, from a long ways off. I heard my Granny hollerin'. The only thing I didn't truly know if the sign from God was for me to go to Granny or to stay away, but I figured I had come pretty far and so I might as well finish. I got up and went toward the sound of and pretty soon I could see a group of three trees in the distance. I knew that it was on one of them that Granny was tied.

The moon was shining through the clouds by the time I got near enough to see her, an until the day the earth swallows me up I'll never forget seein' Granny tied up on that tree. She looked like something from the nitemares I got after smokin' bad dreamy-weed. She was yellow, not a pretty sun-flower yellow, but a sick piss-dark yellow, with open sores from head to foot. Even as far away as I was, maybe fifty feet, I could smell her, like piles of boar shit mixed in with rotten meat that had been sittin' in the hot sun.

The worst part for me was the way she was all swelled up. She was swollen from head to foot, makin' it hard to tell where just one part of her stopped and another started. She was just sorta one big mess of whimpering yellow stinkin' and quiverin' goo. The more I looked at and smelled her, the more scared and sick I got. I felt so bad that I had to see her like that and how there was nuthin' I could do, and then all of a sudden she started to talk.

I'll never figure how she could see or talk to me since I don't think she really had any eyes or mouth left. Sumtimes I try to tell myself that she really wasn't talkin' to me, that maybe she was jus talkin' crazy stuff to herself, but, well, the stuff she said shure sounded like she was talkin' to me.

"Hep mah," she started sayin', slow and quiet at first.

"Granny?" I said. "Granny, it's me, tell me how I can—"

"Ah Gah pleaz hep mah!" she said, louder and with more hurt in her voice. I started cryin', not cause I'm a baby or anythin' but because I couldn't help her.

"Just tell me how I can help you Granny, jus tell me how," I pleaded. She mumbled something that I couldn't understand, so I plugged my nose and moved even closer and that's when it all happened.

"Oh God Oh God jus help jus help jus help!" she hollered in a voice so loud and clear that it sounded like it was comin' frum somewhere else. I realized what she meant or at least what I thought she meant, so I swung the axe meanin' to cut the ropes which were holding her, but instead I sorta hit her and that's when she exploded.

I don't know how long I was passed out, only that when I came too the moon was already halfway down in the sky. I jus layed on the ground for a few minutes, my body pretty much hurtin' all over. I finally sat up and noticed I was covered with yellow sticky goo all over, which I guess was stuff that used to be Granny. I looked over at the oak tree where Granny used to be, but there was only a few strands of rope and a lot of the yellow goo

Maybe it's wrong, but as I got up and ready to leave, I didn't feel bad about what I did. In a way, I think maybe that's what she wanted. I figured at least she wouldn't be in anymore horrible suffering like she was. All these thoughts made me feel a little better as I went lookin' for my axe, and it was when I found it that I got my second sign from God.

Next to the axe was Granny's little finger. Not all swollen and yellow, but just a regular finger. Maybe that doesn't sound like a sign from God, but it was on that finger that she wore a ring, a ring with a small piece of gold in the center, and I remembered Granny tellin' me more then once that the gold was from a mine in the Dakotas.

Rite then and there I decided it was time for me to make my move. I wrapped up Granny's finger real careful in a piece of shirt I tore off, placed it in my pants pocket, and headed off to the West. I know the Dakotas are a long ways off, maybe even a hundred miles, and I know that I'm gonna miss my Ma and Pa and even Honey-gurl, but I guess I realized that in his own way my Pa was right about God jus watching us, seein' what we will do and if we will make the same mistakes. I figured my Pa made a mistake by not leavin with Ma when they was younger to find their own place. Maybe God won't send down the hollers anymore, least not on me. I shure hope so, and I also hope deep down that if he does send down the hollers on me, that one of my kin will do the same for me as I did for Granny.

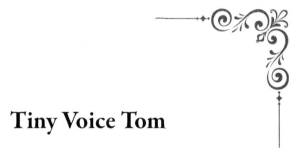

Tiny Voice Tom

Shaun Avery

S haun Avery writes dark fiction in a number of mediums, often with a satirical slant, especially with views towards media and celebrity worship. You can find out more at http://www.comicsy.co.uk/dbroughton/store/products/spectre-show/ and https://transmundanepressblog.wordpress.com/2019/03/17/the-fictionals-origins-by-shaun-avery/.[1] His favourite sub-genre of horror is, of course, body horror, and he is greatly looking forward to everyone meeting . . . Tiny Voice Tom.

---

1. https://transmundanepressblog.wordpress.com/2019/03/17/the-fictionals-origins-by-shaun-avery/

He slid bloody fingers inside her, opening her up, making her wet.

Mary writhed against the memory-foam mattress, pushing herself further down onto him, careful not to nudge Tom's dead body out onto the floor.

This feels wonderful, she thought.

And well worth the wait.

It had started a few months ago.

The voice, in the night.

She'd thought at first that it was just Tom snoring.

But then she'd heard words coming from within there.

"Let me out! Please! I'll treat you much better than he does!"

Which wouldn't have been too difficult. Once proud of his appearance and thoughtful about the upkeep of the house, Tom had degenerated into a total slob. Worse, he never wanted to touch her sexually anymore. Which would have been fine if it was just a case of his libido diminishing over time. But Mary had recently found his stash of old-school porno mags, tucked away behind the cupboard. And they looked pretty well-thumbed.

And sticky.

So when she heard what the voice was saying, it didn't take her long to visualise what life with a better Tom could be like.

Because she still loved him, that was the tough thing. Or rather, she loved the memory of what he used to be. The times they'd had. The sex they'd had . . . and those memories were why she couldn't just kick him out, why she had no desire to find someone else. No, she still wanted Tom. Just not the way he was now.

She looked at him one night, waiting for him to go to bed, for him to sleep, so she could hear his other voice.

The voice that told her nice things.

The voice that came from Tom's throat whilst he slumbered, speaking through the snores. Telling her how gorgeous she was as she lay there naked next to him. She'd never had to do that in the old days . .

. she'd always worn a nightie to bed, back then, and nine times out of ten Tom would end up taking it off with his teeth. Now she slept in the nude in some hope that her bare flesh would reinvigorate him, spread passion through his widening body. But looking at him now, sitting in his chair by the window, it wasn't hard to see why their sex life had gone so wrong. Become so non-existent.

He raked deep inside his nose and wiped his fingers on the arm of the chair.

He picked his feet and left pieces of hard and crusty skin on the floor for her to come along and vacuum up.

His gut hung out over his groin.

Still, Mary could have lived with all of that. She could. She would have been prepared to accept him letting himself go a little. If only he would notice her in some way.

But he didn't.

He didn't even realise that she was watching him now.

Or that she had silently started to cry.

But the other voice noticed.

The other voice cared.

So later on, as Tom slept, Mary lay there naked on the bed once more. And waited.

Until finally it came.

"Let me out of here, Mary," the voice said, "and I'll love you as you've never been loved before."

"But what are you?" she whispered back.

"Another Tom," the voice told her. "A small part of him that's disgusted by what he's become. He tries to deny that I exist. But every time he does that, I get a little bit stronger."

"So can't you take him over?" Mary wondered. "Make him . . . go back to the way he was before?"

"I can't," the voice replied. "I'm still too small. But once I get out of his body – well, then, I'll grow."

"But how will you get out?"

"Easy," the voice said. "With a little bit of your help, Mary."

But she didn't have the stomach for what he then proposed.

So she slept on the couch a couple of times, to get away from the voice.

Tom didn't mind.

"Fine by me," he said, sat there in his usual chair. "I can starfish in the bed."

Mary shook her head at this.

He really didn't give a shit.

But still, she couldn't just get rid of him.

Nor could she ignore the siren call of the small voice. Couldn't forget all of the nice things it had said to her, the promises it had made about how different things would be if she just let it out.

So one of those nights when she'd told Tom she would sleep downstairs . . .

She stood, instead, over him.

A carving knife somehow in her hands.

Her eyes roamed over him.

He had indeed done a starfish on the bed. A huge blubbery mound of flesh, a vast wall of fat. She could barely see the mattress beneath him.

Mary took a step closer to his sleeping form.

She was naked once again.

But she had no sex in mind this time.

Not yet, at least.

Tom snored up at her. Loud and nasal. Like usual.

But from beneath this piercing sound came something else. Something soothing.

"Yes, Mary," the little voice said. "Do it."

And she did.

She drove the knife deep into his throat.

Pushed.

Twisted.

And dragged it out.

His eyes snapped awake, his fingers clutching at the wound, trying to stem the sudden spurt of blood.

Mary stood back.

Her own eyes wide with wonder.

Ears finely attuned, too. Waiting to hear a cry of victory, of triumph, from the little voice she'd now set free. But hearing nothing.

She began to panic.

Had it all just been in her head?

As she wondered this, Tom tried to stand but instead sagged back into the pillows. Blood coming at an alarming rate now. Shooting up and into the air, cascading all over the bed and bedside cabinet.

But not just blood, she now saw.

For tiny hands were appearing through the hole she had torn into his flesh.

She backed off.

Giving him room.

It was a small, featureless form that pulled itself out of Tom's body and slid down onto the floor. But as she watched – and true to his word – the form began to grow. And not just in size but in appearance, too, a face forming there. Tom's face. But not the flabby, unshaven thing she had become accustomed to these past few years. No, a hunky, finely-chiselled visage, with a wide grin and deep blue eyes. Her Tom. A double of the way he'd once been.

And he stood there naked, too.

Her eyes roamed down prominent pectoral muscles and perfect washboard abs to . . .

"Oh!" she said.

"Yes," he said, and walked over and then took her in his arms. "I've been waiting for you a long time, Mary. And now . . ."

He pushed her back onto the bed.

His fingertips – bloody where he had pulled his way out of the inferior Tom – left crimson marks on her bare shoulders.

But Mary didn't care.

The Tom she'd lived with for so long now lay dead next to her.

She didn't care about that, either.

Especially not when his fingers entered her, opened her. And especially not when his penis – thick and hefty and hers, all hers – soon followed.

This is perfection, she thought. This is bliss.

She told herself that it would never end, that this was the start of a new golden age that would last forever.

But . . .

Eight Months Later

She sat on the floor and delved deep into the vacuum bag once again.

Wondering, as she always did, how one man's toenails could be so thick and filthy. And so reluctant to leave the bag, too – clinging in there when she emptied it out into the dustbin, making her go through this rigmarole every time.

Meanwhile, Tom – new Tom – sat in the chair by the window, eating a pizza. Or at least nominally eating a pizza – most of it was hanging from his face. Yet more was splattered all across the arm of the chair. Along with a couple of stringy and gross green snots.

Watching him, she supposed the honeymoon period was over.

And what a period it had been! Sex every night – she'd stopped buying nighties, a particularly virile Tom ruining them with his teeth in his haste to get at her body beneath the fabric. And then there were the compliments, and the back rubs, and the foot rubs, and the flowers, and the running her bath for her, and the buying her little presents since he had all of Tom's memories, and, perhaps more importantly, knowledge of his bank card pin number. This was the same money that he used to pay towards all of their joint nights out – the restaurants, the clubs, no more sitting in the house staring out of the window for this version of Tom, thank you very much. Which meant new clothing for them both – out with the slobby, food-stained T-shirts and in with nice new suits for him, whilst Mary upgraded to nice dresses and sparkly shoes in place of the comfortable stretch-pants and fuzzy slippers she had spent most of the last few years in.

It had been like falling in love all over again.

With one or two practical concerns along the way, of course.

Like getting rid of the original Tom's body the morning after his unfortunate demise.

Well . . . more like afternoon, really. That was when they finally stopped having sex and looked towards the body.

They were in the corner of the room, having just engaged in some rather vigorous action against the wall. Now Mary placed her bare feet back down on the ground and said, "I thought he'd just disappear or something. Now that you're here, I mean."

"Nah." He flashed that wide grin of his again, exhibiting teeth shiny-white and perfect, though she noticed one of her pubic hairs wedged between a couple of them. "That's not the way it works, sweetheart."

"Oh." She frowned. "So what are we going to do with him?"

"Let me take care of that, babe," he replied. "All I need's a saw, some black bags, and a shovel."

"Shovel?"

He looked at her. "So I can bury him out back."

She wasn't sure she liked the sound of that. Knowing he was out there. Every time she went to hang the washing out in the summer.

But what was the worst that could happen?

What could possibly go wrong?

Besides . . .

She trusted her new man.

So she got him the things he needed, then went out shopping for the day.

And when she got back, she found that the original Tom was gone.

The bloody sheets, too. She never saw them again. But she assumed they were buried out back with the body.

As for the blood splattered all across the wall beside the bed . . . well, decorating soon took care of that. Performed in the nude, of course, neither of them able to get enough of each other's naked forms. And in-between their crazy nights out.

But all of that still lay in the future.

For now – on the day after the new Tom's birth – he came up behind her and laid his hands upon her shoulders.

"All done, babe," he said. "We'll just have to wait a little while and rinse the bathtub out again."

Mary wasn't sure she wanted to know why.

But not giving her a chance to brood, new Tom soon had another surprise for her.

He led her out into the front garden, where there was a pile of rubbish laid out in the middle of the grass.

No, not rubbish, she saw when she got a little closer. Magazines. The old Tom's stash of porno magazines.

Mary looked back at her new love.

"I know how much they bothered you, babe," he said. And held up a box of matches and some lighter fluid. "And I know I'll never need them. Not when I have you. So, you want to do the honours?"

"Oh, Tom," she replied, tears coming to her eyes.

It had been some fine love they had made that night.

And every other night, for about the first five months.

But then, following a whirlwind of social interaction and intense sexual activity . . .

"I'm too tired tonight, love," Tom said. "Can't we just stay in?"

"Of course," Mary told him, and secretly she was relieved – she'd been tiring a little of nights out, too.

But she should have seen the signs.

That was how it had started with Tom Mark One, too.

And now here she was.

Picking out his fungal toenails from the vacuum bag. Watching him stuff yet another pizza slice into his face. Unable to stop noticing his widening girth. And not in any of the places that mattered, either.

Mary sighed.

But still, she gave it one last try.

"Tom, honey?"

He looked at her.

Cheeks red with pizza sauce. Slices of meat hanging from them.

"Fancy an early night?"

He looked at her blankly.

Belched.

Said, "Nah."

And grabbed another pizza slice.

She returned to the vacuum bag. Waited for him to go to bed. To go to sleep. Then headed upstairs after him. Stood over his sleeping form. Waited. Waited. Until she heard the small voice say:

"He doesn't treat you right, Mary."

She nodded.

"But I would."

And she smiled.

She wasn't going to wait so long this time.

Mary looked down at his starfish-shaped body, giving one final thought back to the wonderful five months they'd shared before any of this had happened, before he had reverted to form. And wanting more of those good times.

But . . .

Looking at him, she suspected it might not be as easy this time around.

Though his stomach had clearly grown – caused, she suspected, by the sudden halt in their love life, not to mention his new-found appreciation of pizza – he still had a little muscle there and was nowhere near as fat and flabby as his predecessor had been. Which might make it a little bit harder to open to him up. To let out another new Tom who would treat her better.

But not impossible.

Mary nodded to herself once more, sizing up the target.

Then went downstairs to find herself a very big knife.

"Onion"

J. Danielle Dorn

S he received a B.A. in psychology from the University of Rochester in 2007. Her debut novel, Devil's Call, was published by Inkshares in August 2017.

That tattoo had been a bad idea since the moment Mason got it.

Esther's idea, like every borderline antisocial idea had been Esther's. *Oh honey, why don't we getting matching ink for our anniversary?* Esther was covered in ink, every paycheck she earned pulling espresso shots and flirting with businessmen and police officers going straight to her skin, it seemed. Reds and blues and greens, flowers and dragons and anchors, places she had traveled and places that did not exist. And then there were the piercings. Some of them were hot and a few of them freaked him out, but that was Esther. A punk rock chick with pink hair and an attitude problem. He loved her enough to think yeah okay maybe one tattoo won't hurt. He had exactly zero at the time he let her drag him into the parlor where the scruffy artist with bad teeth had seen every inch of her body. Said artist had looked Mason up and down, his appraisal broadcast without words. He thought Mason was a pussy.

It went on the inside of his wrist, so not only did it hurt like hell but complete strangers felt the need to comment on it when he would check them out at the library where he worked. He was one of the few male librarians in the county, and he ended up stuck on desk duty more often than he would have liked owing to his young age and recent acquisition of his Master's degree. He tried to keep it covered. Sleeves didn't always cooperate and some people he could have sworn stared at other people's wrists with the intention of catching sight of a secret. Or maybe he was projecting. Mason was forever noticing other people's scars and tattoos. He was neither brave nor curious enough to point them out.

Not his patrons, though. The younger ones were always exclaiming, asking whether it hurt (yes) or whether he had any others (no) or whether the library let people have visible ink (and piercings! It was 2020, the library board was doing an excellent job of keeping up with the times!)

So when Esther dumped him, out of nowhere, citing irreconcilable differences and his mounting resentment, Mason was the first to admit the shock of it made him lose his mind a little. It wasn't like they were cohabitating and planning on getting married and having lots of tow-headed little germ bags. Still: they saw a lot of each other, and then they didn't see each other at all. Esther dumped him, and the next he knew, thanks to the power of social media, and their priding themselves on their maturity, their ability to no longer date while continuing to follow each other every place a person could follow another online, she was out in San Francisco with her new girlfriend, taking selfies in front of bridges and posting photographs of neon-lit raves and redwood forests. All sorts of adrenaline-seeking outdoorsy shit he would have done with her if she had asked him to.

He had to admit part of the problem must have been that Esther always had to be the one to ask. He had a lot of time to think after she left him. His friends busted his balls, of course. That's why they were his friends. They figured he was holding up well enough in the weeks after the breakup that they didn't need to check in on him as frequently as they had when it first happened.

He could have blamed what happened on alcohol. On the fact that he didn't drink, so his body couldn't handle the impact of it, let alone the volume. It wasn't like he would have done what he did sober. Shifting the blame, though, wasn't something Mason was used to doing. Mason was used to taking responsibility for his fuck-ups.

Cutting off his own tattoo was a level of fucked up he couldn't have blamed on alcohol even if the bottle of Jameson he drank all by himself had attained sentience and somehow managed to wield the blade itself.

He remembered nothing of the lead-up to the actual operation, and he came to after he had made the first cut, a surgical patient resurfacing from the anesthesia unsure of what was going on or why. He had taken a paring knife out of the drawer in the kitchen and laid his arm down on the countertop like a slab of roast he was preparing to trim the fat off and the next thing he knew the blade was bit down through his skin and blood was oozing out of the wound's parted lips and he figured well, he was going to have a scar, he might as well finish what he started.

The worst part was the lack of pain. The hurt he had felt when Esther left, the sense of loss and betrayal and hopelessness, it seemed to dissipate the more he carved away at his arm. He didn't cut deep enough to sever a tendon or an artery with his dull mistreated little knife. Just enough to loosen the top few layers of epidermis, to slice off the patch of skin that held a permanent reminder of the relationship he had had and lost.

When he regained consciousness in the morning, the kitchen looked like he had murdered someone the night before. His wrist throbbed beneath its hasty dressing. He began to fear infection. He began to fear other people's reactions were he to confess what he had done. Normal people didn't carve themselves up when they were drunk. That was disturbed behavior performed by disturbed individuals. He would have to talk to a therapist, start picking at his relationship with Esther, go down the long awful road of examining why he had done what he had done and worrying he would do it again in the future. He couldn't find the ragged square of skin he had removed from his arm. He must have thrown it in the trash while the blackout still had its hold on him.

Hiding the wound was the next hurdle. He managed to clean and bandage it well enough that a button-down shirt could conceal all but the edges of the bandage. A tattoo was one thing. White gauze was another. Anyone who noticed the bandage kept the observation to themselves. Mason began to think he had gotten away with it. So long as no one said anything, he could pretend it hadn't happened.

Yet he had gotten a taste of something dark, something delectable, and he found himself thinking about what it was he had actually done. And as the wound scabbed over and the skin repaired itself, leaving behind shiny new scar tissue, he felt an itch he could not ignore. Like being so horny he had to disappear for a few minutes to tend to that sensation of need.

He was sober when next he took the paring knife to his body, this time higher up on his forearm where the flesh was tender and taut across the muscle. This time was different. So soon as the blade broke the skin a shiver of sated hunger rippled through his nervous system, up his trunk and down into the pit of his belly, and there was not quite so much blood as there had been when he was pickled on Irish whiskey. Science was looking out for him that day, and the thought occurred to him that maybe if he could slice away all the skin that Esther had laid her hands on, then he could exorcise her from his life. Regain his sense of peace. It wasn't a conscious thought so much as it was a feeling, an impulse. And removing tiles of his own skin felt good enough that it seemed worth trying. It wasn't like the flap of skin he had sawed off the first time hadn't healed. It wasn't perfect, but he wasn't after perfection. This was as close to burning away the past as he could get without dying of smoke inhalation.

He refined his technique with each session. The preparation became a ritual, cleansing and centering himself, and he began to treat his tools with the care they deserved rather than grabbing up the first thing he found in the knife block. He spent a few hours on the Internet researching knives one night only to find scalpel components in a bookbinding catalogue at work the next day. They called to him from the pages, and he ordered a ceramic handle and a box of blades. He went to the drugstore the day the package arrived to pick up rubbing alcohol and triple antibiotic ointment and gauze. He put together a kit, not unlike the bag his college roommate Sandro used to have for shooting heroin.

It wasn't fair to compare what he was doing to what Sandro did. Sandro had gotten addicted to narcotics after a skiing accident his senior year of high school, and his doctor had cut him off halfway through undergraduate. He had turned to heroin to keep from going into withdrawal during finals, and the last anyone knew he was still shooting up. The fact he had landed a job in the fashion industry while harboring a habit like that astonished everyone in their cohort more than anything else. If Sandro could make a life for himself while punching holes in his body with a syringe, the rest of them had no excuses.

The scalpel bit in a way the paring knife hadn't, sharp and competent, designed to do this kind of work. Paring knives were made for removing the skin from apples, the cores from pears. Not for attaining a state of ecstasy courtesy of careful self-mutilation. And Mason was careful. Starting at his wrist and moving his way up his arm ensured that by the time short-sleeve weather arrived, the scarring on his forearm was more or less uniform and it looked as if he had suffered a bad burn, not a self-inflicted renewal. When he reached his elbow, he took off the skin on the back of his forearm. The hair did not grow back.

Mason had thrown the first few patches of skin away, figuring they were evidence of his nascent disturbance. They were casualties of the cleanup process, his goal to remove the blood and gore from the place where he kneaded pizza dough and chopped vegetables. It seemed to him a shame to toss the patches by the fifth or sixth one. He didn't know what else to do with them. Then he realized sticking them to the pages of his day planner would cause them to dry there like the skin was attempting to graft itself to the paper, a last desperate bid to stay alive. Of course, it didn't, and as time passed and he flipped past the page the skin resembled a stain more than an actual bit of living flesh that had once been attached to his body. But it was nice, he thought, to be able to see the chronological progression of his ritual, to look at the skin within the context of time and remember the exact date, the exact time, that he had sat down to work on himself.

When the time came to deglove his right hand, the demarcation between new skin and old too apparent for him to ignore and his brain insistent that he commit to the spirit of the exercise, he had to wear a medical apparatus designed for people who were recovering from similar injuries. He had researched that on the Internet as well, before he actually went ahead and did it. Spent an hour hopping from one gore website to the next, fascinated by the body's ability to withstand injury and horrified by the comments anonymous individuals left behind. Like using Sharpie to deface a bathroom wall.

People stared at the glove more than they had ever stared at the tattoo, but they did not comment on it. They minded their own business. And while that hadn't been the point of the exercise, it was an added bonus that brought Mason comfort. Patrons he saw on a regular basis kept the conversation to the books they were checking out or to their own problems. Once his right hand was healed enough that he could flex his fingers again, he got to work on the other arm.

Spending all that time on the Internet looking at knives and bloody injuries gave Mason an idea of where to go for his next inquiry. No matter how skilled he was getting at removing his own skin, he wouldn't be able to get the place Esther's hands spent the most time. She used to love raking her fingernails down his back when they were in bed together. She massaged his shoulders as a preamble to asking for something crazy, to seducing him, to opening a bottle of wine and packing a bowl and spending the night at his place only to slip out the door when she finally reawakened in the afternoon. He was going to have to pay someone to take the skin off for him. He was going to have to pay them to keep quiet about it later. While he embarked upon that search, he started in on his chest and abdomen.

The person who answered his posting on the message board went by the handle razorxclarity and signed their private correspondences "clare," every letter lower-cased. Mason wasn't able to find out much about this person from plugging their handle into search engines. It didn't matter to him whether it was a man or a woman, so long as they got the job done.

At least, that was what he told himself. The person who agreed to meet him at the lonely motel off the highway the next county over, assuming that was the same person who actually showed up at the motel, turned out to be a statuesque young woman with icy blue eyes and a square jaw. She was plain yet poised, and for the first time, Mason feared for his own safety. Like she could do whatever she wanted to him and he would agree. She carried an old-fashioned black physician's bag and wore black leather driving gloves.

"You've got the money?" she asked as soon as the door was shut behind them.

"On the dresser," he said. Like in the movies, he didn't say. Her lips quirked in a smile anyway. Like he had told a joke that made her want to groan instead of laugh.

"We're just doing your back?"

"That's the part I'm having trouble with."

"Let me see what you've done so far."

That request took him by surprise, but he didn't suppose he could begrudge the artist the opportunity to compare techniques, or whatever it was she was doing with her request for consent. Mason took off his shirt and tossed it, inside out, over the back of the cheap desk chair. Clare's eyes moved over his chest and arms, and as she looked him over she slowly tugged her fingers free from the driving gloves. Her hands were long and slender, her nails trimmed and unpainted. She set the gloves down on the dresser by the envelope of cash.

"You cut off your nipples," she said.

"I did," he said.

"That's a major erogenous zone."

"I'll be alright without them."

Mason laid down on the mattress like he was there to receive a massage, arms folded beneath his head and feet dangling off the edge. The splashing chill of isopropyl alcohol sent a hard shiver through his body. That this was a pleasure was obvious. He wondered if Clare had met anyone like him before. He tamped down that thought before it could go much further. Of course, she had. Clare was like Esther. Fearless. Fearless women had no need for wimps like him.

"You brought ice?" she asked.

"It's in the bathroom."

"Want to talk about why you're doing this?"

"Not particularly."

"Good. No offense, but I hate it when guys try to turn this into a therapy session."

"I think I'm a bit beyond therapy, at this point."

"Heh," Clare said.

She snapped on a pair of nitrile gloves and stood over him on the bed. She did not sit down. She sure as hell did not straddle him. This was not a kink session where they were going to use safe words and engage in aftercare. It was a business transaction, and Clare was going to work quick and clean, and they were going to go their own happy separate ways afterwards.

The first incision sent another shiver through him, and Mason turned his face away from Clare out of... what. Modesty, shame, guilt. A puritanical reaction Esther would have mocked him for, like experiencing sexual arousal as a result of painful stimulus was something he had any control over. It wasn't like he could only get off by envisioning little kids or watching videos of women crushing small mammals beneath high heeled shoes. There was a spectrum of deviant behavior. At least Mason's was only hurting himself, and 'hurt' was a bit of a stretch.

"Alright?" Clare asked, her concern as detached and clinical as the rest of her.

"Yeah," he said.

"It's alright if you cum. I'm not going to judge you."

Her forthrightness startled him, and he almost turned his head to look at her again, but she was back to cutting, making one long perfect line from the top of his left shoulder blade down his ribs, following the border created by his previous solo efforts. At home, by himself, he was only capable of small patches of skin. He knew how much he could cut before he couldn't control the bleeding. Whatever Clare was doing, with her pressure and her application of mystery tinctures, he would never be able to accomplish on his own. It was making his heart beat faster, and he had to exert more self-control than he had thought himself capable not to grind his hips into the mattress.

He had no way of knowing if she was lying when she said she would not judge him. He wasn't going to ask her to stick around to clean up. That he climaxed as she cut the sheet of skin free from its fascia was none of her business. She left him clotting on the bed to drape the skin over the ice bath. He could hear her moving around in there, clicking on the light with her elbow and jostling the shower curtain.

When she came back, it was to dress the wound. She recited a litany of instructions, awful similar to the ones Mason had had to follow when he got inked, with the reminder he now had a big open wound on his back. He had to treat it like the potential infection that it was.

"I'd be more than happy to check up on you," Clare said. "Once a week, say, until it's healed. Unless you want to take your chances with your primary care doctor."

"What's the going rate for back-alley wound-care specialists these days?"

"Don't call it back-alley. This is pretty clean for a shit-bag motel."

So it went for the next several months. Mason used vacation time, then personal time, while he ate antibiotics with every meal and saw Clare every Wednesday night to make sure the antiseptic showers and ointment dressings were doing their job. He wanted to keep his project going, could see, and even worse, feel places on his body that retained the memories of Esther's hands. But Clare urged patience. She reminded him that the dermis sheds, that he would have had a whole new set of un-scarred skin within six weeks anyway. That at this point he had to realize this wasn't about Esther. He had awakened something in himself that he liked, but he was afraid of it, so he blamed it on his ex.

"I thought you said this wasn't therapy," he said as he pulled on his shirt after their last session, where Clare declared his back a giant scab that was free of infection and on its way to scarring.

"It's not," she said as she clipped her physician's bag closed. "I'm just saying, you're running out of things to flay that aren't going to majorly affect your life. Are you planning on degloving your penis? What about your scalp? Your face? This isn't some cleansing ritual, man. It's... I don't know what it is. It's none of my business, is what it is."

"The rest of it I can do on my own. You don't need to worry about what this is."

"You're a grown man. It's your body. You can do what you want with it. But own your shit, if you're going to keep going. That's my un-solicited advice."

That was the last time he saw Clare. She gave him a long, somber look, framing him alive in her memory before walking out the door for the last time. A part of him wanted to call her back. To tell her he had thought a lot about what she had said to him over the course of the last several weeks, that he wanted to get off the path he was on.

But he didn't. And he didn't.

He got to work on his legs, emboldened by Clare's procedure. He took off the skin on his right thigh in two sheets, then managed to un-wrap the entire left thigh in one go. His lower legs were easy. His feet, nothing compared to taking the skin off his hands. He did them both at the same time rather than letting one heal before skinning the other. No one could see what he was doing to himself underneath his clothes. He didn't spend enough time standing at the library for anyone to re-mark upon it, although by the time he reached his soles his coworkers and the patrons had stopped asking him questions anyway. Something was wrong, and they knew something was wrong, and the fact that he smiled and lied and kept on showing up for the evening shift offered

absolution to people who would have done something if there was anything they could have done.

Standing naked in front of the mirror in his bathroom the day he
unwrapped his feet for the last time, slathering vitamin E oil over his
body as he always did, Mason did not feel the sense of completion he
had thought he would. Clare's question bounced around the inside of
his skull, reminding him of the places that still retained their original
skin.

He sat down to write a letter the night he decided shaving his head
wouldn't be good enough. He did shave his head, first with the closest
setting on his electric razor and then with a disposable pink one Esther
had left behind, scraping free every hint of follicle he could. It would
grow back. He no longer had hair on his arms, his chest, his legs. Even
his toes and knuckles were bare. In its place was shiny, perfect scar tissue, tougher and newer than the skin it had replaced.

Removing his scalp was easy, once he set up the mirrors over the
sink to allow him to see his head from all angles. Once he got the bleeding from his hairline under control, the hot red fluid soaking into the
gauze instead of running into his eyes. He lost track of the number of
times he climaxed. The nerve endings in his head reacted as if they had
never been touched before he cut them, as if Esther had never made a
habit out of running her fingers through his hair, massaging his scalp
after a long day at work. By the time he was finished, the sight of the
glistening red dermis was enough to slake his thirst. At least for that
night.

The termination notice he received from the library came in the
middle of that year's use of sick leave. Something about the board members having to think about the effect the librarians had on patrons'
peace of mind, what kind of message they were sending to the community, they were willing to work with him to resolve his personal issues
but he needing to take the first step, and so on. His supervisor had tried
to call him dozens of times, and he knew damned well she had. She

wanted to discuss specifics. She wanted to address his emotional health, to have him come in for a meeting to "have a chat." Nothing good ever came from sitting down to "have a chat" with the person responsible for signing his paychecks. So he let them fire him. He filed for unemployment insurance. It would help him pay the rent and his bills while he saw this through to the end.

His scalp healed as he knew it would. He had a bit more trouble with the skin between his legs. It didn't have long bones beneath to offer stability, and it was so thin and delicate that he cut deeper than he meant to in places. It bled in a way he found difficult to control.

In the end, he decided he didn't need the organs he couldn't skin anyway. It was like trying to peel a grape. The skin was part of the fruit. He learned about banding and ordered the equipment from a farm and ranch supply website. By the time the tools arrived, scar tissue had grown to cover his skull. It was smooth and insensate, with no sign of hair. For the first time since Esther left him nearly a year earlier, he felt close to completion.

The morning came when he awakened to find the bands had done their jobs. Blackened masses of unrecognizable flesh separated from the front of his pelvis with a few twists of his wrist. He stood before the mirror a priest before a shrine, exultant and aware of what he needed to do next. The stubble on his jaw, the hair on his brow. The lashes on his eyelids. It had to go. It all had to go.

The Big Bad Boy

Patrick Winters

Patrick Winters is a graduate of Illinois College in Jacksonville, IL, where he earned a degree in English Literature and Creative Writing. He has been published in the likes of *Sanitarium Magazine*, *Deadman's Tome*, *Trysts of Fate*, and other such titles. A full list of his previous publications may be found at his author's site, if you are so inclined to know: http://wintersauthor.azurewebsites.net/Publications/List

Here she was, only a half hour into her Friday night shift, and Maisie already had a gun pointed to her head.

As if that weren't bad enough, she'd just peed herself, and the tears were starting to tingle in her wide eyes as she stood there, rigid and terrified behind the checkout.

"Do what I say and I promise I won't hurt you!" the ski-masked gunman shouted. But to Maisie, the dire urgency in his voice—and the way the revolver shook in his hand—didn't match up with the promise. She managed to nod, anyway, hoping to Heaven that he was telling the truth.

A sudden rumble sounded out in the Dollar Stop and Maisie jumped, shutting her eyes and squealing through gritted teeth, thinking the gunman had just broken his promise and taken a shot at her. But when she realized she was still standing (and breathing) the truth of the noise sunk in. It hadn't been a gunshot; it was a harsh roiling coming from the masked man's big gut.

He certainly wasn't the usual type of crook you'd see, at least not on those late-night cop dramas. They were always gruff-voiced and thin, lithe and able to make quick getaways. This one sounded youthful and nasally, and he was portly—to the extreme. Maisie figured his pants were a size 42, at least. They looked awfully tight about his ample waist. His pudgy hand engulfed the grip of his gun, his trigger finger stuffed into the frame, and the skin about his eyes and mouth puffed out from under his strained mask.

The gunman's stomach gave another growl, as though the Native American on his poor football jersey was trying to speak to them. The man bent over in discomfort as the grumbling drew out, the seams of his dark jacket actually splitting as he cringed with his pain. But he kept his gun on Maisie, in spite of whatever was wrong with him, and he barked at her again.

"Get out from behind there! Now!"

Maisie flinched as he shook the gun in emphasis. Her limbs finally loosened, letting her scurry out and around from her station. The gunman took a few lurching steps her way as she crept forward, his bulk swaying like a pendulum. He kind of reminded her of one of those fertility goddess statues she'd seen in her World Civ course last semester; the comparison could have almost made her laugh if she wasn't busy soaking her leggings again.

"Please, don't . . ." Maisie began, but she couldn't finish the sentence. "Wh- what do you want?"

She'd been right by the register, but he hadn't demanded she open it. So, if he wasn't after money, then what was he after?

"Over to aisle six. Move it!"

Maisie scurried around him as he lowered the gun, holding it at waist-level. He followed after her as she headed for the aisle of bread and snack cakes.

She stopped in the mouth of the aisle, dozens of mascots from Little Debbie, Sunbeam, and the like smiling at her misfortune from their packaging.

"The Little Devils," the gunman said. He nodded down towards the center of the aisle, where that brand of sweet was arranged on the Dollar Stop's shelves. Maisie hurried over to them and then turned around to face the gunman. She shrugged at him, lost to her fear and her growing confusion.

"Grab them!" he said, jutting his gun out at the snack cakes. "The Big Bad Boys. Hell, all of them!"

Maisie looked at the dozens of Little Devil boxes before her. The cartoon Satan stamped across each of them grinned at her, winking and promising that the product was "Devilishly Delicious!" The Big Bad Boys—newer cakes, triple-layered with crème—had much tubbier devils on their boxes, rubbing their bellies and declaring the cakes to be "Sinfully Scrumptious!"

In that moment, Maisie's surprise trumped her fear, and she turned back to the gunman. "You're robbing us for junk food?"

"I don't wanna eat them!" the man yelled, making her shrink back. "I wanna burn the bastards! Get rid of them! And you're gonna help me. Now, start grabbing!"

The revolver's barrel swung back to her, and Maisie started reaching for the boxes, snatching them up and cradling them in the nook of her arm, squeezing and holding as many against her chest as she could manage while the gunman began a rant.

"There's something seriously wrong with those things! Those fuckers have ruined my life! And others'. I know they have! But no one understands; no one believes or pays any attention. They just look the other way while the people who make this shit keep doing it! They . . ."

The gunman started to cry just as Maisie dropped some of the boxes. She ducked down onto her haunches and picked them up again, then went for the ones on the lower shelves. She spared glances up to the gunman as she grabbed; he paced nervously about the aisle, his gun aimed lazily at the floor.

"The same shit happened to my cousin! And a college buddy! They went to the hospital, got checked out, ran tests—but the doctors couldn't explain it! I went when it started happening to me, and they couldn't help me, either! Asked if we'd been out of the country, or if we were exposed to something. Radiation, or some shit like that—fucked if I know! But we hadn't been. No way. So they asked if we were allergic to anything."

The gunman gave a humorless laugh and reached a hand up to his mask. "Does this look like a fucking allergic reaction to you?"

He pulled the mask off his head, revealing scruffy black hair and a round, red face underneath. And not just red—practically scarlet, the bulge of his cheeks and the folds of his forehead livid with the color. His ears, nose, and lips were puffy and raw, and while Maisie had seen similar swellings with allergies, this seemed incredibly extreme for that.

The whole effect made his head look like a balloon filled with blood—a balloon on the verge of bursting.

Maisie turned away from him, not wanting to get too good of a look at him, should he realize that his hostage could now identify him without his mask—and besides, he wasn't exactly pleasant to look at without it.

She kept grabbing at the Little Devils as the man continued on with his crazy explanation of things.

"Then my doctor asked what I'd been eating lately. Said maybe I had something that didn't agree with me! I'd say so! It was these god damn snack cakes! I just know it was!"

The gunman kicked out at a box that had just slipped from Maisie's grasp, sending it flying to the end of the aisle. Maisie whimpered but kept on with her task, her arms nearly full now, the corner of a Big Bad Boy box jabbing up into her neck.

"I'd just started eating them when this began happening to me. And my cousin and my buddy had done the same! I asked and they said so! Gina tried them a few weeks before me, and Tyler just one or so. And then when Gina—"

The gunman stopped as his stomach gurgled and churned again. He groaned in pain and set his hands to his knees, huffing as his gut eased itself once more. When he spoke again, it was through more tears.

"And then Tyler a few days later. It was awful! No one knew how it happened. No one realized it's these fucking cakes that caused it! I told them, but no one believed me! Sure, it sounds crazy, but you know what's crazier?"

The man reached his free hand into his pocket and brought out a phone. He thumbed it and stepped over to Maisie as she stood up with her haul. He shoved the phone in her face, showing her a picture of some guy. He held a beer in his hand and he was smiling wide. He was probably about her age. Lean, thin-faced, not entirely handsome, but definitely decent. He had scruffy black hair and was wearing a very baggy jersey with a . . .

Maisie gawked at the photo, not sure if she could believe her eyes.

"Yeah, that's me," the gunman said. "From just two weeks ago."

He flicked his phone off and returned it to his jeans. He raised his gun again as he waddled back and away from Maisie.

"Those fucking cakes did this to me and my friends. I don't know how, but they did. And if no one can or is gonna help me, I can at least try and stop it from happening to others. I bought my cakes from this store, so we're gonna burn all that you've got, here and in the back, and you can never sell these things again! And then I'm gonna—"

Another grumble from his stomach sounded off like distant thunder. The man doubled over again, his arms wrapping around his belly as he screamed in pain.

"Shit! No! It's happening. God, no . . ."

He looked up to Maisie as he started panting, jabbing one of his sausage fingers towards her. It seemed to her that he was growing redder by the second—and was it just the light playing tricks, or was his face actually . . . getting bigger?

"You have to get rid of those, no matter what!" the man cried. "Burn them! And tell others! Stop people from eat—"

A shrill yell cut into his plea and he arched his back, his whole body going rigid with a spasm of agony. Maisie moaned and took a step back, realizing that, yes, he was getting bigger. His fingers were puffing up; his neck was spilling out of his jersey like a cake rising in an oven; his raw belly was peeking out and over his jeans; and she could even hear the fabric of his clothes tearing and snapping as he just continued to expand.

He screamed again, and Maisie joined him. Then his jersey and jacket ripped open—and so did he.

His skin and his fat ballooned out from his bones until the pressure was simply too much, his flesh splitting all over; and in a literal split-second, the gunman was gone in an explosion of blood, torn clothes, and human bits. A spray of red splashed over the tiled floor, along the aisle—and all across Maisie. Her scream became a choked gag as she felt the man's warm, sticky blood wash over her arms and her face like a wave, bits of bone-shrapnel pelting the boxes she held and fleshy chunks sticking themselves in her auburn hair.

Maisie stood there a moment, frozen and horrified, watching as a scarlet mist dissipated in the air.

As the meaty pop the man had made rang itself out of her ears, she let the splattered Little Devils fall to the floor. She started shaking her arms, trying to get the blood off as another scream rose up and out of her.

Maisie ran, leaping over the pile of soaked clothes and jumbled human remains that were in her way, her sneakers squeaking along the slick floor. She bolted for the store's doors, flinging them open as she went screaming into the night.

The Dollar Stop grew quiet again, save for the drip-drip-drip of ruined items in aisle six, and the Little Devils the man had wanted destroyed grew soggy in the spreading pools of his blood.

Revenge of the Toothfish

C.M. Saunders

C. M. Saunders is a freelance journalist and editor from south Wales. His work has appeared in over 80 magazines, ezines and anthologies worldwide and he has held staff positions at several leading UK magazines ranging from Staff Writer to Associate Editor. His books have been both traditionally and independently published, the latest release being a collection of short fiction called X3: Omnibus

After gunning the engines through the night, they finally reached the fishing grounds and dropped anchor. The instruments told the crew they were currently just above a shelf, the total depth being 1,800 feet. A few hundred feet away, the shelf dropped off into the abyss. The depth there could be a couple of miles. This area was deemed a prime location.

The Carolina was a small boat, only eighteen-feet long, and so carried a small crew. On this particular outing it was just Captain and boat owner Hans Strommer, two designated fishermen Sam and Henry, and deckhand and general dogsbody Alfredo. It was a 'low-key' fishing expedition. Everyone was very careful not to use the word 'illegal.'

They were after Patagonian toothfish, a cold-water species more popularly known by its more palatable 'dinner table' pseudonym Chilean Sea Bass, and would be using rod and line. These fish were too big and aggressive to be caught in nets. It wasn't unusual for them to grow up to six feet in length and weigh over 200-pounds, but just one good-sized specimen could be worth over $2,000 at market. The first catch gutted, headed and dumped into the converted freezer in the hold covered fuel and other expenses, anything they caught after that was pure profit. They hoped to return with a thousand pounds or more, which would mean a nice little payday.

They had to be quick about it. The longer they stuck around, the more chance there was of them being discovered by the coast guard and ordered to produce papers they didn't have. That could lead to all kinds of fuckery. There was so much red tape involved in the industry, the lot of a modern-day commercial fisherman wasn't a happy one. "In and out in two days," the skipper said.

So far so good.

Though Patagonian toothfish were the prize, the Carolina was an opportunistic vessel. Sometimes she caught other things. Sharks were common. If they were small and the meat not worth the storage space, Captain Strommer ordered their fins to be lopped off for sale to the

Chinese restaurants and the rest either dumped overboard, still bleeding but unable to swim, or chopped up into pieces and used for bait.

Otherwise, like now, they baited their hooks with the sardines they brought with them. Most of the fishing was left to Sam and Henry, who managed two or three rod and lines each while Alfredo baited the hooks and did all the fetching and carrying and Captain Strommer concentrated on making sure everything ran smoothly from the wheelhouse atop the cabin. Every member of the crew knew that this translated as keeping watch.

The first hour passed painfully slowly. There were a few tentative bites and nudges, but nothing to shout about let alone reel in. The fish were down there alright, they just weren't taking the bait. Then, just as they were discussing chumming the water again, Henry had their first bite. "C'mon, fucker!" he yelled, jerking back his rod to sink the hook deeper in the fish's mouth and wincing with the effort as the carbon fibre bent almost double. The muscles beneath the yellow SLEEP, EAT, PARTY, REPEAT t-shirt the man wore strained and bulged with the effort.

A few minutes later, the small crew was gathered on the Carolina's tiny deck. In front of them, the fish Henry had caught writhed and squirmed, smearing its own blood and shit on the floor. It appeared to be ten or twelve pounds and was covered in thick jet-black scales. Its bulbous head, accounting for almost two-thirds of its body, boasted a huge protruding yellow eye on each side, and its gaping mouth was a mass of sharp, pointed teeth. The strangest thing about it was the clumps of coarse brown hair sprouting out of its body.

"What the fuck is that?" Sam said.

"It's a fish," Henry replied, deadpan.

"Don't be a smartass. I been fishing twenty-two years and I ain't never seen a fish like that before."

"Might be some kinda catfish or something?" Alfredo suggested.

"Or it may be a fish new to science," replied Henry. "Everyone thought the coelacanth was extinct until some fucker hooked one in 1938. All kinds of mad shit happens at sea. You just don't get to hear about most of it."

"Ugly lil' bastard, ain't he?" Sam said, upper lip curling in disgust as he leaned in for a closer look.

"You ain't no oil painting yourself," Henry said, a little defensively.

"Yeah, well. Whatever it is, it's not much good to us," Captain Strommer said curtly. "Unhook it and throw it back where it came from."

"But what if it's a new species?" Henry argued.

"Do you wanna explain to the authorities what you were doing out here and how you came to catch it?"

"Guess not," said Henry, stooping to pick up the fish. He gathered it at the third attempt and, holding it still with one oversized fist, wrapped the line around his other hand and pulled. The hook came free with a little spurt of blood. That was when the fish leaped from his hands and launched itself at its handler. Henry screamed as the creature buried its teeth deep in his cheek. "Get it off me! Get it off!"

Captain Strommer, Sam, and Alfredo all took a step back. To a man, they were as shocked as they were horrified. Henry was twisting and turning, arms flailing. He was in danger of falling overboard. He was trying to grip the fish to pull it off his face, but it was too slippery.

"Gerroffmeee!" Henry's voice was now muffled. He was choking on his own blood.

"Fuck! Okay, okay, hold it right there!" Sam swung a right hook as hard as he could. It landed with a wet slap, sending Henry flying across the deck. He landed on his rump, arms splayed behind him, with a look of utter confusion painted on his face. As if as an afterthought, the fish relaxed its grip and fell to the floor, either stunned or dead.

"Why did you hit him like that?" Alfredo said.

"You have a better idea?" Sam snapped. "That thing was eating his fuckin'face!" He took a short run-up and booted the fish as hard as he could. It sailed through the air, clipping the handrail as it went, and landed in the sea with a plop.

Henry hadn't moved. He sat on the deck, eyes glazing over. His lower face, along with the front of his SLEEP, EAT, PARTY, REPEAT t-shirt, was covered with blood and gore. He was trembling. Sam knelt next to his companion to inspect the damage while Alfredo peered over his shoulder, swallowing hot bile as it tried to rise in his throat.

The entire right side of Henry's face was a mess. The damn fish hadn't just bitten him, it had gnawed him. There was a hole in his cheek so deep Alfredo could see the white of his teeth through it. Jagged flaps of skin hung from the wound, which still oozed blood.

"You okay?" Sam asked.

Henry said nothing. He just stared.

"What's wrong with him?" Alfredo asked.

"Got bit by a fuckin' fish, that's what's wrong with him," Sam said without turning around.

"I mean, why ain't he saying anything? Or even screaming. That's gotta hurt like a total bitch."

"Prob'ly in shock," Sam said. "Either that, or the damn thing injected him with some sort of venom."

"Venom?"

"Similar to what mosquitos use, I guess. Part painkiller, part anti-coagulant. Or maybe even something stronger which numbed or incapacitated him."

"Don't care what the hell it did," Captain Strommer said. "Can't have him just lying there like that. Help him below, will you Sam? Put something on his face, then come and get back to work."

"Okay, skip."

"Meantime, Alfredo? Congratulations. You just got a promotion. Grab a rod."

"But what if I catch another one of them... things?" Alfredo said hesitantly.

"Do you want the promotion or don't you?"

"I s'pose I want it?"

"Then shut up and grab a fuckin' rod."

Sam returned a short while later, his face ashen. "He's in a bad way," he said. "He's delirious and running a fever. We should get him to a hospital."

Captain Strommer regarded the crewman with a look of pure disdain. "We can't go back yet. We haven't caught us a single toothy, which means we're a couple of thousand bucks in the hole. We're not going anywhere 'til we make this trip profitable, so I suggest you get fishing. Sooner we fill the freezer, sooner we can get outta here and get him some treatment."

Muttering under his breath, Sam took up his rod. Like Alfredo, he knew the skipper was too stubborn to do anything other than what he set his mind to.

By mid-morning all they'd caught was a dogfish, which they threw back, and captain Strommer was getting increasingly tetchy. He kept disappearing into the wheelhouse to look at the charts and instruments, giving Alfredo the impression he was thinking about moving out to another fishing ground sooner rather than later. He was on one such mission when Sam and Alfredo first heard the moans from down below.

"Sounds like that painkilling venom's wearing off," Alfredo said.

Sam looked irritated. "Go see if he's okay, quick before the skipper comes back. I'll keep an eye on your rod."

Alfredo lay his rod against the side of the boat, the line still dangling in the water, and hurried down the short sequence of steps leading below deck. At the bottom of the steps was a door leading into the main cabin-cum-galley. He pulled it open.

Henry was lying on one of the benches, his lower half covered with a thick woollen blanket. He looked terrible. His flesh looked bloated, his clothes were drenched with sweat, and the wound to his face still oozed blood and puss. His eyes were opened wide, as if in a permanent state of shock, and his skin was deathly pale, so much so that in places it looked almost grey. Was he suffering some kind of infection? Or an allergic reaction?

When he saw Alfredo standing in the doorway, he called his name.

"I'm here," Alfredo replied, unsure of what else to say.

"Water," Henry said, sounding as if he had a throat full of phlegm. "Water."

Alfredo went to the cooler where they kept the bulk of their supplies, unscrewed the cap off a bottle of Evian, handed it to Henry, then looked on dumbfounded as rather than put it to his swollen lips, he tipped the bottle up and emptied the contents over his head.

"The fuck are you doing?" Alfredo said. "Have you lost your mind?"

"More,"

"More water?"

"Bucket."

"You want a bucket of water."

"Yesh." Henry gazed up imploringly at Alfredo from his bed.

"Skipper won't be happy if you start tipping all our drinking water over your head like that," Alfredo reasoned.

"Thea water. Pleash."

Alfredo couldn't believe what he was hearing. "You want me to get you a fucking bucket of seawater?"

"Yesh! Pleash!" As Henry spoke, spittle flew from his engorged lips and he thrashed his head from side to side on the sodden pillow.

"Okay, okay," Alfredo said in his best soothing tone. "I'll get it." He ran back up the steps and onto the deck. He heard either the captain or Sam shout something but he pretended not to hear them, and didn't turn around. He knew there was a bucket fixed to a rope there used to rinse down the deck. Finding it, he quickly lowered it into the sea, let it fill with water, then took it back to Henry.

"Give it. GIVE IT PLEASH!" the stricken man cried when he saw the bucket, holding out his hand weakly.

Face twisted into a grimace, Alfredo hurried over to the bed and passed Henry the bucket. This time, he did drink. Holding it with both hands, he fixed his swollen lips to the side of the bucket, tipped it up, and poured it down his throat. The salt water bubbled and frothed down his chin, soaking him.

"That's gonna make you..." Alfredo began, his words trailing off when he realised he was too late.

"More," Henry said, thrusting the now-empty bucket in Alfredo's face.

"N-no, man," Alfredo stammered as he took the now-empty bucket back. "You don't know what you're saying, or doing..."

"I SHEED MORE!" As Henry opened his mouth to yell, a jet of vomit shot out of his mouth, hitting Alfredo in the face. He was no expert but he supposed it was technically vomit because it came from inside him, but it was mostly sea water. He could taste it on his lips, and it was still cold.

Coughing and spluttering, the young deckhand held up his hands and backed away, "Okay, man. Whatever you say." Closing the door behind him, he went back on top deck, picked up his rod, and resumed fishing.

"How's he doing?" asked Sam.

"Not too good. Looks like shit."

"Worse than he normally does?"

"Oh, yeah."

"Why are you all wet?"

"Fucker done threw up all over me."

"That's pretty gross, kid. You aren't gonna go wash that shit off?"

"Not much point. It's mostly fucking sea water."

"Please yourself. He was drinking that?"

"Yup."

"The fuck didn't you stop him?"

"I tried. He wasn't havin' any of it. Sicked everything back up, anyway."

It didn't take long for the sun to dry Alfredo's face and clothes. As he fell into the rhythm of fishing, he did his best to block out what had happened below deck. He was largely successful, too. It was hard work maintaining two rods.

Sam had moved to work on the other side of the boat, and Captain Strommer constantly moved between the two, cursing and complaining. "The fuck are all the toothies doing today? I know they're down there. Try chumming some more. Use different bait. Feed out more line, fish deeper. Do something. Anything."

Nothing they did made any difference. As morning turned to afternoon, the converted freezer in the hold remained empty. Alfredo began to think Henry had passed out. It was all quiet below. Until it wasn't.

"WAH! FUG WAH! GIM FUG WAH!" It sounded like poor Henry was trying to talk through a mouthful of cotton wool.

"What's he yelling about?" Captain Strommer asked, irritated.

"He wants more water, Skip," Alfredo said.

"Didn't you give him any?"

"Sure I did, he drank it. He wants sea water, sir. Want me to go see to him again?"

"He wants what?" the captain grumbled. "Fuck's sake. No. You stay on those rods. I'll sort him out myself."

Captain Strommer disappeared below deck, leaving Alfredo and Sam to carry on fishing. Almost immediately, Henry stopped shouting, which Alfredo took as a good sign.

How wrong he was.

It was another ten or fifteen minutes before Sam spoke up. "It's gone real fuckin' quiet down there."

"Better than listening to Henry calling for water all the time."

"True. Go see if everything's okay."

"Do you think I should?"

"Just said so, didn't I?"

Alfredo really didn't want to go below deck again. His last visit had creeped him out, and since then a bad feeling had settled over him. He knew nothing good could come of it. Even so, Sam was right. He should go and see what was going on. Either Henry or Captain Strommer might be in trouble.

The smell was the first thing he noticed. He'd caught whiffs of it when he was up on deck, but dismissed it as a natural result of working on a fishing boat. But here, it assaulted his nostrils with such vigour that it made his head spin. It was the smell of fish after it's been out of the water a while. But that wasn't all. Beneath the fishy veneer was the stench of rotting meat, and beneath that was another. This third component was harder to pin down. It was metallic and coppery, yet also earthy and organic. Alfredo didn't know what it was until he opened the door.

Blood.

The walls and even the ceiling were splattered with it, and pools of the stuff lay on the floor. It was already congealing and turning a dirty brown colour. Captain Strommer lay in the far corner. Or, more precisely, what was left of him. It looked like he had been torn to pieces, reduced to a pile of body parts. His decapitated head lay on top, one eye wide and staring, the other socket an empty void.

Henry sat on the edge of the bench.

Except that wasn't quite right.

It wasn't Henry anymore. Some awful, monstrous abomination had taken his place. The clothes it once wore had been discarded. All except the yellow SLEEP, EAT, PARTY, REPEAT t-shirt which was now pulled tight over a huge, bloated body. The skin was now almost black and appeared to be covered in thick, scaly protrusions, while its arms had metamorphosised into short, skeletal, translucent appendages. Fins.

Worst of all was the thing's face. Though it still retained some of Henry's features, it looked like they had been grossly manipulated or re-arranged somehow. Its yellowing eyes were way out of proportion and had realigned themselves so they were on opposite sides of the head. The nose had elongated and extended into a snout, and the mouth was ringed by a pair of bulging, dark grey lips.

As Alfredo looked on in horror, the lips parted and the Henry thing spoke to him. Or tried to. All that came out of its mouth were a series of wet slurps and smacking noises. The mouth had too many teeth. Sharp, and pointed, they crowded for position, overlapping and protruding. After an extra-loud vocalization, the Henry thing toppled off the bench and onto the floor of the cramped cabin, where it writhed, twitched and spasmed.

Alfredo has seen enough. Turning on his heels, he ran back up on deck. "Sam! Sam!"

"What?"

"It's Henry!"

"What's he done now?"

"He turned into a fish and killed Captain Strommer!"

Sam actually threw his head back and laughed at that, holding his rod with one hand while he slapped his knee with the other, tears rolling down his face. "That's a good one, kid. You have a sense of humour, ya know? You're funny. Weird as fuck, but funny."

"I'm not kidding, Sam! He turned into a fish!"

"Don't be so fucking stupid. How could that even be possible?"

"It was that... thing we caught today. It bit him on the face, remember? It must've done something to him. Changed him."

"Well, if he really turned into a fish, we'll stick him in the freezer and sell him at the market. Probably be the only thing we'll be able to salvage from this whole trip. "

"Don't say that, Sam. It's Henry!"

"No, it's not. It's a fucking fish. You just said so yourself."

"Not completely a fish. Not yet, anyway. He's down there breathing air. He must still be... transitioning."

"Would you listen to yourself?"

"I know it sounds crazy, but how else can you explain what's happening to him?"

Just then they both heard a crash so loud it rocked the boat. It was coming from the cabin. Their heads snapped around in unison. "Did you close the door?" Sam asked.

Alfredo shook his head. "I figured a giant fish wouldn't be able to get up the stairs, anyways."

"It can jump up the stairs like it's trying to do right now. Wouldn't be able to open a door, though. No hands."

"Well, I'll remember that for next time," Alfredo said.

As if to prove Sam's point, there was another enormous crash and the bloated, blackened Henry thing flopped on to the deck where it lay on its side, mouth agape and bulbous yellow eyes staring. It still wore the SLEEP, EAT, PARTY, REPEAT t-shirt, though it was now stretched so tight it was beginning to split. Throwing his rod to the floor, Sam began to back away. "What the fuck is that?"

"I told you! It's Henry. Or it used to be Henry. What are we gonna do, Sam? What are we gonna do?"

"I'll show you what we're gonna do," Sam said, skirting around the Henry thing. "Keep an eye on it."

"I won't take my eyes off it," Alfredo replied. And he didn't plan to.

The Henry thing looked exhausted. Climbing steps without legs must really take it out of you. It might also be dying. Even if it was once a man, there was only so long a fish could survive out of water. Its sides heaved, and its mouth opened and closed as it gasped.

He wondered if the Henry thing retained any human sensibilities. Did it now think like a fish? Or was it still a man, now trapped inside the body of a fish? If that were the case, it must suck.

"Henry?" he asked hesitantly. "You in there?"

No reply.

He'd hoped Henry thing might acknowledge him somehow. It didn't. There was no recognition whatsoever. That disappointed Alfredo slightly, but what did he expect?

Suddenly, Sam appeared from below. He caught Alfredo's eye and put the fingers of his left hand to his lips. In his right, he carried something. Only when he pointed it at the Henry thing did Alfredo realise it was the flare gun they carried in case of emergencies.

"Sam, no!"

"You got a better idea?"

"We can just help him back into the sea."

"But he killed the skipper. Did you see? Fucking tore him up into little pieces."

"Oh yeah," Alfredo conceded. "I forgot about that."

"Never liked the fucker, anyways. Always thought he was a better fisherman than me. Well, I'm about to show him once and for all who gets the bigger fish. Stand back."

Sam pointed the flare gun at the Henry thing, turned away to protect his face, and started applying pressure to the trigger.

Alfredo backed away.

That was when the Henry thing burst into life once more. It flexed and contracted every muscle in its sleek, lithe body, then leaped high into the air, thrashing its tail for added momentum. Alfredo watched, helpless, as the giant fish opened its jaws impossibly wide, and engulfed Sam's head. Sam tried to scream, but the scream was cut off and reduced to a muted, muffled sequence of pitiful gurgles. As the Henry thing snapped its jaws shut, the noises stopped.

The force of the huge fish slamming into him propelled Sam toward the safety railing, pin-wheeling his arms in a fruitless attempt to maintain his balance. As he and the Henry thing toppled over the edge, the flare gun went off, shooting a fiery projectile across the deck and into the cabin. Then, the whole world was suddenly consumed with choking smoke and blinding phospherant.

For a moment, Alfredo stood alone on the deck watching the fire burn, a million thoughts cascading through his mind. Everything was moving so fast. He knew what would happen when the fuel tanks ignited, and he didn't want to be around when they did. Sucking up a huge lungful of air, he dived over the side. As he hit the water, he heard the explosion.

Treading water amongst the wreckage he looked around for another boat. There wasn't any. He hoped the smoke would attract someone, but they were well away from the shipping lanes and the sea was a big, big place. It would be getting dark soon.

Then something brightly coloured caught his eye. It was Henry's SLEEP, EAT, PARTY, REPEAT t-shirt. It reminded Alfredo of something Henry had said earlier that day.

All kinds of mad shit happens at sea. You just don't get to hear about most of it.

Dead Cert

Roger Jackson

Roger Jackson has had several pieces published in small press magazines, as well as a number of short stories broadcast on UK radio. He's had short stories published in several anthologies, such as Equilibrium Overturned from Grey Matter Press, The Flashes of Darkness e-book from Dark Chapter Press and the Manifest Reality anthology from Hair Brained Press. He is pleased to say that the anthologies have been well received, with his own contribution being mentioned favourably in reviews. He have another seven short stories scheduled to be published this year. Additionally, his novella "Cradle of the Dead" was published by Bloodbound Books, and again has received a positive response in reviews and on social media.

She was staring at her reflection in the hard silver skin of the juke, dreamily unmoored to the wiry, leather-jacketed stranger staring intently back at her. The stranger's image curved weirdly across the polished shell, distorted and distant, as though she was seeing it in some fairground hall of mirrors. She saw a half-child in monochrome warpaint; beneath the tangled spill of stormcloud hair, her eyes were ringed with black, glinting dully like dirty glass, hollow orbs tattooed with living ink on the inside, pupils and irises and lacework veins. Tonight, she decided, the stranger's name was Stacey.

She selected the last of her three tracks on the juke and punched in the numbers. The first of her chosen 45s was plucked from the ranks and flipped on to the turntable. A moment later Patsy Cline commenced serenading the breathing shadows in their smoke-fogged booths, singing about how crazy it is to love somebody. Stacey turned and walked slowly back to the bar, sensing his cold, insectile gaze crawl hungrily over the swell of her breasts beneath her black t-shirt.

He hadn't changed much in the last eight months. He was perhaps twenty-five or so, tall and muscular, sporting the same stubbled scalp as his companions. He wore the right jeans, the right trainers, and the football shirt of his team. They all did, just as they all drank the same beer and shots and smoked the same brand of cigarettes and leered stupidly over the same vacuously pneumatic models and pop stars.

When she'd walked in alone from the night and the sky's promised tears he'd whispered something to his mates and oh how they'd laughed. It was then that she'd turned and made eye contact, held it for that all-important extra moment, the one he'd read as Yes, come on over. Talk to me.

She'd sat at the bar and ordered her drink from a claret-haired woman whose tired smile told her a lot. Whiskey and lemonade. The taste was cloying on her tongue but she drank it down and ordered another. Let them think she was in the mood for something sweet.

They were watching her now, filtering her presence and behaviour through a murk of male intuition, thinking with their scrotums, their sour cargo the only grey matter that mattered to them. If a woman's alone then she's waiting for a man. Fuck off and die means she's playing hard to get, or she's frigid, or she's a lesbian. She imagined their conversation about her, full of lewd speculation and so-called compliments wrapped in dirty silk.

Nice tits ...

Bet she bloody gives it away ...

Yeah, she's a dead cert ...

She watched him for a few more minutes, in the long mirror behind the bar. Watched his companions goad and cajole him into making a move. Watched him and waited. She didn't wait long.

He slithered up behind her, fed her some chat-up gambit strewn with cobwebs – it wasn't Do you come here often? But it was close – and offered to buy her a drink. Smiling, she accepted. The second of her jukebox tracks was on now. Cheatin' Heart. He offered her a cigarette. Again, she accepted and smoked it slowly. If nothing else, she knew she gave good filter. They talked for a while. He asked her a few impersonal questions she gave him the answers he wanted to hear, knowing he'd never remember them anyway, the way he didn't remember her. Twice during the brief conversation, he forgot the name she'd given him.

Eventually, he said, "My car's just outside."

She never did get to hear that last 45.

THEY STOOD IN SILENCE in the car park in the rain. She felt cold and soul-dead, her flesh as drained as a wrung-out rag. The world around her was a dirty, metallic grey. Colourless neon rippled and swam in the puddles at her feet. Grey thoughts in her head. Grey memories of a grey job in a grey factory, cutting small parts for some vast, unknown machine. Grey threads in her hair, though she was only young, she thought. Grey dreams.

"So," he said. "Your place or mine?"

"No." she told him. "Here. Now."

He half-smiled, surprised ... and maybe a little scared, she thought. Good.

"Erm ... okay, right." He held the rear door open for her and grinned unpleasantly. Stacey felt her revulsion uncoiling. She had a sudden, barely controllable urge to shatter that grin into a handful of enamel splinters.

Instead, she got in.

Sliding across the back seat, she caught sight of herself in the rear-view mirror. Her make-up had bled in the rain; behind the damp tangle of her fringe, her eyes were clogged with mascara tears, sunken grey moons in decaying orbits. They were naked now, it seemed; the stranger was gone. Quite suddenly she remembered a seventeen-year-old girl she had once known, taking a short cut home one winter's night, across the waste ground that bordered the estate where she had lived. The girl had known she was taking a risk, the stretch of forbidden desolation was unlit and deserted, a landscape of burned out cars and reeking vegetation erupting through ancient concrete, of ruptured refuse bags and discarded condoms. She had been scared, scared of the dark and the silence, but not as scared of these things as she was of getting home late, of causing her Mum and Dad to worry.

Stacey found herself wondering if she would ever remember what became of that girl, but then the man was scrambling on to the back seat beside her, his bulk squeaking against the cheap vinyl. She turned, hitching up her skirt and holding him in a dual embrace, like a spider, arms folded across his meaty shoulders, stockinged legs wrapped around his hips. Her hands ran through his wet hair like curious mice. He squeezed a hand between their bodies, unzipping and sliding his blunt fingers the length of her thigh. He meant to hook her panties aside, she guessed, his bloodshot eyes widening when he realised there was no need.

"You're cold," he breathed hoarsely. "I'm cold, too. Let's see if we can't warm each other up, eh?"

Stacey didn't answer and he didn't seem to notice. When he tried to kiss her his breath reeked of beer and stale cigarette smoke and she turned her face away. He didn't seem to notice that, either.

His tongue probed her ear like some squirming, eyeless worm as he held her open and guided himself to her. Stacey felt him pause momentarily, perhaps wondering if he should use some protection but deciding to chance it anyway, after all, if she ended up with a kid it wouldn't be his problem would it and only gays caught AIDS didn't they –

God Above, she wanted him dead.

He pushed himself a little deeper, cautiously, frowning as though something within her was blocking his way. She smiled and drew her legs back, pulling him in all the way in one sudden movement; sour air hissed between his teeth, pain or pleasure, she didn't care. Finally, inside, he whispered a name that wasn't hers.

And stopped.

She felt him half collapse inside her, his lust stolen by the unnatural chill of her. "What -" he had time to say.

Her hands tightened suddenly against his skull, the blackened fingernails slicing his scalp like razor blades. He snarled and tried to snap his head back but Stacey was stronger, stronger than she looked and stronger than him. She pressed her cold lips to his and he screamed against her mouth, thrashing between her legs and clawing frantically at her hands. Stacey felt nothing. He tore at her clothes, and she found it right that it wasn't drunken passion that drove him now but terror. Now she might start to enjoy this. His fingers seized a handful of her hair and pulled; it came away in his grip, strands of black and grey. He clawed at her face, make-up, and meat peeling away beneath his fingernails.

Her tongue, somehow sinewy and slimed with filth, squeezed between his teeth and in horror and shock he bit down on it. It burst in his mouth, ejecting its payload of eggs laid in dead flesh. She heard his cries, choked and choking, and felt a wondrous savage joy bloom inside of her.

He struggled for a time and then was still. Stacey disentangled herself from his remains and got out of the car. She could feel her tongue in tatters behind her teeth but knew it would heal.

She reached into her jacket and took out her own cigarettes and lighter. She leaned on the car and smoked, listening to someone else's choices play on the jukebox. Her cigarette was only half done when she decided to flick it away, watching it arc across the dark like a shooting star, and only hearing its whispered death in a pool of dirty water.

Skin-Deep Monsters

Kiki Gonglewski

Kiki Gonglewski is a senior at Albuquerque Academy high school. She was a finalist in the 2017 state-wide "NM Girls Make Movies" screenplay contest, has won a National Medal for Scholastic Art and Writing, and received 8 gold keys in their Southwest Regional levels. She has also been published in the 2018 edition of Navigating The Maze, an international teen poetry anthology, literary magazines Gypsum Sound, Unfading Daydream, and Third Flatiron's most recent anthology, "Terra, Tara, Terror!"

You looked human, once. Handsome, in your younger days, with a red heart pumping blood so clean and crisp and thin you hardly felt it. But now it struggles, oozing thick and black like molasses under your once-skin. It was witchcraft that did this. It must've been. Bit by bit, the scars began to taint the little pieces of you, so slowly that at first, you dismissed them as coincidence, unable to make the connection. But as your skin began to boil, and the corners of you began to gradually rot... you slowly noticed a correlation. No sooner had you hurt some-one, your fingertips withered like sun-dried apricots. You tortured an-other, and your blood turned thick and black inside your veins. Every wound on any of them...translated into another boil, another scar on you. Witchcraft. Voodoo. Someone must have cast a spell to make you a living, breathing Dorian Grey, with no picture to hide it. And every day it's worse. Bloodshot eyes sinking deeper into bruised, purple sock-ets, the scars atop your skin rising horribly like yeast for all the world to see.

And the solution is laughably obvious— just stop the hurting, the killing... and you'll be plagued with no more deformities. Perhaps there was once a time you could have turned back... But the dormant-self that went with it, one that perhaps would have found such culprit-ac-tions despicable in the first place, has not stirred in years. Stop? It's out of the question. Instead you find yourself hiding it, under longer and thicker sweaters and jeans. You begin wearing gloves, wide-brimmed hats, large sunglasses, scarves in the middle of the summer so they stay hidden behind concealing clothes and cellar doors. You've always done such a good job at disguising yourself over the years, even before this slow and sickly transformation of the flesh. Back when you were hand-some and young and red-blooded, your smile was so brilliant and love-ly that no one ever found themselves looking down at your hands to see the lingering stains within the crevices of your palm, or the crust-ed iron that you didn't quite manage to file out from under your nails. No, people were stupid— and very shallow. Easily bought, never even once suspecting. Why, they'd follow a pretty smile anywhere—and indeed often did on a whim. Why not? Stepping inside for a cup of tea or refreshments didn't seem like such a big deal after that. Perhaps, from a random bout of neighborly generosity, you had bought a present for them, or perhaps you had something (renovations downstairs, was it?) you'd like to show them if they'd only step in for a minute. Tourists, lost, did they say? Well, you had a map inside. If they'd just come on inside, inside...

But you don't smile anymore. Your charming smile that many once followed straight into your house and down into your cellar like the irresistible magnetism of the pied piper's music is gone. Over the last few months, your yellowing teeth have begun rotting from the inside out. Lips, thin, cracked and ridden with sores and boils, can now only stretch over them to create some ghastly leer. So nowadays, people tend to go missing in the dark occasionally. Men who grew in the habit of taking long, solitary walks at night, or the wretched drunks that accidentally wandered too far away from their debauched flock within the haze of a ruinous stupor, or marauding youth on the way to or making a hasty escape from egging some rival's house, and—if business is slow— a stray dog or two. Brute force has never been your strong suit, but you've no choice but to evolve alongside yourself. No more smiles or siren's songs.

But people are so very shallow, and appearances are the first and often last thing they ever observe and take to heart. They may not have truly seen you before, but once the small flaws started to creep their way upwards and outwards onto your skin...it's as clear as day. It would make no difference whether or not they were a testament to your actions. Regardless, you know exactly what conclusions they'd draw. So wide-brimmed hats, gloves, scarves, sweaters do the trick for now.

The challenge grows daily. Keep it hidden, concealed underneath lengthening fabric now that some damned malevolent curse has somehow made it break the surface of your skin. Even now, they vocalize their concern for your wellbeing of late. At first, their voices were tinged with curiosity, but lately, suspicion. They can't seem to tell you're deteriorating from the outside in—even from the small uncovered portion of your face and your lips and your once-skin and the lack of your once-smile? No, not yet. All they see is an eccentric man, hiding under heavy winter clothes when summer's heat is in full swing. You try not to care. Better that than the alternative. And better than, then to stop altogether. But no matter what happens, they can't ever know, see what you see when you look in the mirror. Work of the devil, you are. They'd all turn against you in a heartbeat. They'd have themselves a necktie party, or burn you at the stake...

No one ever found the bodies—you made absolutely sure of that. But since the curse, that no longer stops them from coming back to you as hideous creatures in the shadows, in the corners of your eyes, or pressed up against the inside of your skull. They haunt your life. A crowd of them will follow your excessively clothed figure, damp with heavy perspiration, when you dare risk walking outside. At home, they line the walls of every room, lurk in hallways, or wait in closets, along with the myriad of disassembled body parts you find in cupboards and pantries and drawers until you dimly remember what horror feels like. Even in your sleep, they've managed to seep through into your dreams to turn the tables on you at long last. Sometimes, they whisper to you, seething words in ugly shapes. At others, you hear their shouts and screams, while another disgusting deformity appears on your skin to match what you've done. And your coal heart beats faster and louder as it pumps ink-black blood and weakly-recalled electric fear all through your once-body, a ruinous shadow of itself, and you can't help but feel burning indignation at such a transformation even though you know it is no less than you deserve. What have they done to you? They populate your world like some hideous cancer, so many of them, so many... you'd forgotten there had been so many. But now, they've all rushed back to remind you, swarming your every waking moment with bodies as disgusting and broken as yours. And you scream, "Monster! Monster!" but not to them. For you were human once— no more.

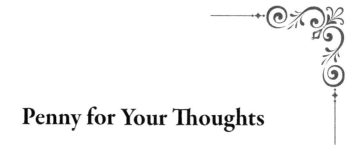

Penny for Your Thoughts

Jacinta M. Carter

J acinta is a college English professor, but all of her time outside the classroom is spent reading everything she can get her hands on. She has always had a slight obsession with serial killers (much to the horror of her friends and family, all of whom are tired of hearing about murder) and include them in many of the stories she writes.

"My father used to save pennies." I turn the small circle of copper over in my gloved palm. "If we behaved, he'd let my brother and I count them."

I hear a groan from the bound mass on the floor, but I have no interest in him yet.

"When he died, he left me $8,220.41 in pennies." I toss the coin from one hand to the other. "He left my brother nothing."

The whites of the man's eyes glow in the dark. He tracks my movements as I circle him, continuing to move the penny from my left hand to my right and back again. Over and over. Finally, when he seems almost hypnotized, I crouch down next to him, my bare feet almost touching his arm.

"You're about to make me two cents poorer."

My Bowie knife makes a shallow cut into the meat of his upper arm. I doubt it's too painful, but he screams against his gag and bucks away from me. His range of motion is severely limited due to the cords tied around his arms, torso, and legs like a straightjacket, but he manages to bend his knees enough to slide almost an inch across the floor.

"Don't make this harder on yourself."

I dig the knife in until blood spills over the eight-inch blade. I grip his arm with my left hand and shove the penny into the cut, temporarily damming the blood flow.

"Now if you'll just hold still, we can get this over with."

I circle him again, tossing another penny back and forth. I allow him to writhe on the floor for a few minutes before squatting down next to his other arm. A series of tribal tattoos decorate the skin between his shoulder and elbow. It would be unthinkable to destroy this masterpiece of ink, despite how cliché they are, so I slide my knife down to the crook of his arm. He flinches though the steel leaves him unmarred for the time being.

The smell of piss permeates the air as I sink the knife into the soft flesh inside his elbow. I roll my eyes, grateful that this won't be my mess to clean up. I give the knife a quick twist and jerk it back out. There's more blood this time, so I hurriedly cram the penny into to wound, stopping up the flow. It's barely past midnight, and he'd ruin my fun if he bled out now.

I wipe off the knife on the rolled-up cuffs of my oversized black jeans and stand up. What little arm muscles he has jerk against his bindings. I don't know if he thinks that he can actually free himself or if it's a completely involuntary reaction, but I laugh at his futile attempts.

"You probably think I'm doing this because my father didn't love me enough." I straddle his torso and sit down heavily on his ribcage, forcing out a cough that smells like whiskey and salami, even with the cloth secured over his mouth. My eyes water a little from his breath, but I swallow down the urge to gag and focus on the task at hand.

His earlobes are attached to the side of his head, a genetic trait I've always considered an oddity. His eyes follow my knife as it passes over his face and disappears just outside his line of vision. The blade slices cleanly through the skin connecting his left earlobe to his head. Despite the blood, this actually makes him look slightly more natural to me. I repeat the process on his right ear, eliciting screams that seep through his gag as he thrashes his head around.

"My father and I were pretty close actually." I wipe the knife on my pants again and check my reflection in the blade. My features are blurred by the smeared blood. "We used to play baseball every Saturday with a few other dads and their kids. My brother came along a few times, but he was more interested in computers, so he usually stayed home."

He smashes the back of his head against the floor and suddenly stops moving. I glare down at him. If he's knocked himself out this early in the game, I'll be furious. Listening carefully, I hear the slight hitch in his breathing. He's trying to even it out, but that hiccup of fear betrays him. He's still conscious. The sneaky bastard.

I lean down until the tip of my nose touches his. He flinches, giving himself away even more. Keeping our faces together, I slide the point of the knife up and nick the skin between his nostrils. His chest heaves as his breathing quickens. The knife pierces the skin, and I dig it in until the two holes in his nose become one. The smell of blood overpowers my senses as I sit back up to avoid getting any blood on my face.

"No, my father was a good man. The only connection between him and my being here tonight is that he gave me those pennies and said to use them if I was ever in trouble. I've only used ten cents from that inheritance so far. Twelve cents, if you count what's in your arms."

His eyes roll back in his head and I hear a gurgling from his throat. His nasal cavity is filling with blood and suffocating him. I usually save the nose for later, but he was pissing me off and I got ahead of myself.

"I'm going to remove your gag. But if you try to scream or call for help, I'll slice off your dick and choke you with it."

He can't give me an answer, but I have to take the chance that he heard and understood. I pull the cloth away from his face and cut through it. He coughs and sputters, a fine film of blood splattering from his mouth. I use a clean place on the cloth to wipe off my own face and then drop the stained rag on the floor beside his head.

"So dramatic," I mumble as he continues to choke on blood, saliva, and possibly a little vomit.

I stand up, grab a handful of his hair, and yank him into a sitting position. He was balding, to begin with, so I'm rewarded for my efforts with a chunk of gray hair, separated at the roots. He bends forward, vomiting blood into his lap and all over the hardwood floors.

"I hope you have a maid," I tell him, stepping back to keep my toes clear of the splash zone.

"Why me?" he chokes out. "Why me?"

I stare down at him, disgusted. "Because I only needed one thing from someone like you. One thing would have saved me and my daughter. But you said no. Every single one of you said no."

He tilts his head back and looks up at me incredulously. Not a hint of recognition in his eyes. Typical. Guys like him never waste a second glance on people like me. I grab the right, size-11 Chuck Taylor sneaker from the carpet where it waits, just out of reach of the blood pool on the hardwood. Eyes still focused on him, I slip into the shoe and lift my foot. His eyes widen in realization less than a second before I smash the heel of the shoe into the remains of his nose.

His body crashes back onto the floor, shaking the decorative plates in the China hutch across the room. I pull off the shoe and toss it back over beside its mate.

The man is lying almost completely still. The only indication that he's still alive is the facial twitch that has developed in his chin. Or maybe he's trying not to cry. I can't tell and I don't particularly care.

"I was going to save this for later, but I've heard more than enough from you tonight." I walk around him and kneel next to his head. He squeezes his eyes shut tighter, so I know he senses how close I am.

With my left hand, I grab his quivering chin and jerk open his mouth. He clenches his teeth together to protect his tongue, unaware that he's making my next move even easier.

I flip my knife around, carefully wrapping my gloved hand around the blade. It took me three types of gloves before I managed to pull this off successfully, but whatever this material is ensures that I don't gash open my own hand. His perfect set of teeth grins back at me, though dulled a bit by the fresh coating of blood. Gripping his chin to steady his head, I bring down the handle of the knife, shattering his front teeth. I repeat this motion three more times in quick succession, knocking loose or breaking as many of his teeth as I can manage before I lose my now blood-slicked hold on his chin.

He tries to roll himself on his side, spitting out fragments of teeth. A solid gold crown shoots out from between his lips, still perfectly intact. I scoop it up and inspect it, fascinated, as I belong to the generation that uses more subtle means of tooth repair. The man starts choking again, so I slam my knee into his back to drive out whatever is lodged in his throat. I absentmindedly slip the gold crown into my front pocket and roll him back over to lie flat.

"I'll let you keep your tongue," I promise, winking conspiratorially at him.

I usually cut out the tongue. It's actually one of my favorite parts. But the tongue is a slippery instrument all on its own, and with the amount of blood already in his mouth, I don't think I can manage to hold onto it without taking off my gloves. Damn him for making me slice open his nose too early!

His arms tense as I pinch my fingers on either side of the cut holding the penny in his left arm. I slip the knife in and work the coin loose, releasing a torrent of blood through my fingers as the penny lands – heads up – in my palm. The penny in the crook of his right arm takes a bit more manipulation before it's free. I wriggle in the knife, hearing it click against the copper and flick my wrist a few times until the edge of the penny pokes out of the wound. It's too bloody for me to see whether I've spun heads or tails on this one, but I place it carefully on the floor next to the other one.

The man groans and it sounds almost like actual words. I lean a little closer to the bloody maw that used to be his mouth and ask him to repeat himself.

"What are you going to do with me?" At least, that's what I think he asks. It seems a reasonable enough assumption.

"Don't worry," I assure him, kneeling with my thighs on either side of his head. "We're almost finished here."

He looks almost relieved and I wonder if he understands that only one of us will leave this house alive. Perhaps he knows what's going to happen to him and has resigned himself to his imminent death. Either way, I still have one more step before I can leave.

I set down my knife next to the two pennies and gently stroke the man's face with my fingers. My gloves are the type made for people who can't spend more than a minute away from their iPhone, so the fingers have more texture than if I'd gone with standard latex gloves. His face relaxes, despite blood still streaming from almost every orifice. I run the fingers of my left hand over the man's forehead, massaging it a little, while my right hand reaches into my back pocket for the two sewing needles I keep stabbed into the fabric of my jeans.

A needle in each hand and no longer touching him, I whisper, "Look at me."

He opens his eyes almost sleepily. Without giving him a second to comprehend what's about to happen, I drive the sewing needles into his eyes. He lets out an otherworldly shriek and thrashes on the floor like a fish who can't find his way back to the water. I squeeze the needles between my thumbs and middle fingers, ratchet them in opposite directions, and yank them up. I hear a satisfying pop, reminiscent of a celebratory champagne cork, and then his eyes are dangling out of their sockets. I pick up my knife and slice through the nerves, releasing their hold on the eyeballs. His left eye rolls down his face and hits the floor with a squishing sound, but I catch the right one and place it gently on the floor.

His body continues to writhe, but I lock my thighs more tightly against the sides of his head, preventing any movement that might interrupt me. I grab the heads-up penny, force my fingers between his twitching left eyelids, and drop the coin into the empty socket. With the other penny, I smear away enough blood to determine which side is heads and then shove it into his right eye socket.

I'm slightly impressed by this man. I honestly hadn't expected him to last so long, especially considered how much the small cuts into his arms made him squirm. But, I have a job to finish, and I can't waste time admiring him.

He is mostly still as I release his head and move back around to his left arm. I retrieve the eye and check it against the gaping wound in his bicep. The eye is slightly too large, so I jam my knife in the hole and twist it around until there is enough room to fit the eye. He makes no noise, but he's still breathing raggedly, so he's likely finally passed out. I step over him and grab his right eye from the floor. The hole in the crook of his arm is larger, so it takes less work to squeeze in the eye, for which I'm grateful.

I watch the rise and fall of his chest, counting the seconds in between. I won't stay until he's completely stopped breathing, but I prefer to remain on guard until the breaths come too far apart for a likely resuscitation.

When the movement of his chest is barely perceptible, I sit back and check the bottoms of my feet. I somehow managed to keep them both clear of the blood pooling around the man's body. I stand up, stretching out my back and legs, and admire my handiwork. Though I feel a little sympathy for whoever has to clean this up, I can't help but smile at how smoothly everything went. Well, other than the fact that he still has his tongue.

Careful to skirt around the blood, I walk over to the carpet and slip my feet into the Chuck Taylors on the carpet. I tuck my knife and the needles into the cargo pocket on the side of my pants and hike them up by the waistband, wishing I'd remembered to wear a belt.

Halfway to the back door, something begins to nag at me. Sighing in resignation, I walk back to the body. I pull my knife back out, bend over the man's face, and reach between his lips. I manage a tenuous grip on his tongue, but it takes no more than a few seconds to saw through, leaving me with about two inches of tongue in my fist.

Based on the lack of reaction, I assume he's either finally dead or his body is paralyzed with shock. I move over a few inches, unzip his jeans, and stick his tongue into the zipper gap. Now I feel that I've truly completed tonight's work.

Without another look back, I stride to the back door, let myself out, and sneak through the backyard to the alley. My car is parked a few blocks away, but I make it there without running into any other night owls.

CASEY WAKES ME A FEW hours later. I've been sleeping on the couch to avoid a fight every time I come in late but based on the continual slamming of kitchen cupboards, it's clear that my absence from the previous night was noted.

I don't have the energy to deal with Casey this early in the morning. I've been persona non grata ever since losing my job a few months ago, forcing Casey to abandon the position of stay-at-home parent in order to go back to work after only two years. We'd been equally shocked when every bank refused to hire someone who'd been a loan officer for over a decade into any position higher than a teller. So now Casey spends hours every day helping little old ladies operate the coin machines in the lobby and explaining to teenagers how to set up their first checking accounts.

Instead of going to the kitchen to beg forgiveness, I sneak down the hall to our three-year-old daughter's room. She's still sleeping peacefully, unaware of the fight about to break out on the other side of the house. Just before I turn away, I notice a faint bruise forming on her upper arm. Anger bubbles in my throat like bile and I stalk back out to the kitchen.

"What the hell happened to Penny's arm?" I ask through clenched teeth.

Casey doesn't even turn from the stove to look at me. "Maybe if you'd been home, you would see that Penelope lacks proper discipline."

"Discipline? Leaving a mark on a child is not discipline! It's..."

Casey cuts me off. "I have to get to work. You get to stay home all day and baby her now, but when I'm here, she has to learn to mind me."

The house phone rings, startling us both. I often forget we even have a landline and can't remember the last time either of us actually used it. Casey is closer and grabs the receiver, barking out a quick hello.

I step toward the phone, trying to hear, but all I have to go on is the look on Casey's face, which is growing steadily more concerned. After listening for a couple of minutes, the phone slips and I manage to catch it just before it hits the linoleum. I hold it up to my ear, but whoever was on the other end has hung up.

"Who was it?" I ask, suspecting I already know.

"Sawyer." Casey's voice is barely a whisper, but it shocks me. If that was Sawyer on the phone... "Sawyer's dead."

I bite the inside of my cheek and swallow down my sigh of relief. "What? Was he sick?"

Sawyer was the head loan officer at Casey's old bank. Sawyer was one of the first who refused to reinstate Casey as a loan officer, leading to the never-ending job hunt that eventually resulted in the dreaded teller position. Sawyer was the man I killed last night.

"Haven't you been watching the news?" Casey spat angrily. "Bankers all over the city are being murdered! Some maniac is targeting loan officers."

I bristle a little at the word "maniac," but keep my face neutral. "Well, it is a job that requires you to turn people down when they're most desperate."

Casey glares at me, practically foaming at the mouth. "Are you trying to justify this? People are dying...My friends are dying, and all you can think about is why their murderer might be doing the right thing?"

"That's not what I'm saying, Casey." It's a struggle to keep my voice even. "But when people are backed into a corner, you never know what they might do."

I put a little extra emphasis on the word "corner" as that's literally where Casey has me trapped at the moment. Before either of us can make another move, the doorbell rings. With a final glare at me, Casey stomps to the front door. I follow as far as the kitchen doorway, wanting to only hear the exchange.

"Can we speak to Mr. Miles, please?" The voice sounds official and formal. I take a deep breath and step into the hallway so the police officers can see me over Casey's shoulder.

"What is this about?" Casey asks, trying to act gruff and instead sounding like a toddler.

"Mr. Miles?" the cop asks, getting a nod of confirmation when he locks eyes with me. "We have your fingerprints at the scene of Michael Sawyer's murder. I'm here to place you under arrest."

I look down at my toes as the officer rattles off the Miranda Rights. The big toe on my right foot appears to have a touch of nail polish on it. I hide my right foot beneath my left as I realize what the color actually is.

"What the hell is going on here?" Casey roars. "You can't possibly think..."

"I'm sorry about this ma'am," the officer says while his partner tries to restrain Casey. "You can follow us down to the station if you'd like, but I suggest you first call a lawyer for your husband."

I look up and catch Casey's eye. We stare at each other and in that moment we both understand that there will be no lawyer. There will be no getting out of this one.

"Let's go." The lead officer nods to me apologetically and his partner jerks on Casey's upper arm.

I stand in the front doorway and watch as my husband is led away in handcuffs.

"Mommy?" Penny asks from behind me.

I close the door and turn to face her. "Yeah, baby?"

"My arm hurts." Her lower lip quivers and her eyes dart around the room. Casey has clearly threatened her with further violence if she reveals to me how her father abuses her when I'm gone.

"It'll be okay, Penny," I assure her. "Let me see it."

We walk into the living room together and I pull her onto my lap. I inspect her arm, but luckily it's not damaged beyond the bruise. I hug her tightly and kiss the top of her head.

"How about some breakfast?" I ask. She nods enthusiastically. "Hey, baby, has your dad been in my pennies?"

I already know the answer before she confirms my suspicions. Though I couldn't be sure he'd take the bait, I'd left one of my coin jars on the dresser where he'd be sure to see it. I knew he wouldn't be able to resist taking a couple here and there. Sneaking two from his pocket last night had been a cinch. And guaranteed they'd have his fingerprints on them.

"Go get dressed and I'll start some pancakes."

Penny runs back down the hall to her room and I walk through the kitchen to the laundry room. The clothes I'd worn the night before, all stolen from Casey's closet, are still crumpled on the floor by the washing machine. His Chuck Taylors sit by the back door, looking as though he kicked them off on his way in. I nudge the right shoe with my toe and check the bottom. The faded white waffle-pattern is interrupted by a smear of dried blood that's taken on a crusty brown hue. Even without the penny fingerprints, there's more than enough evidence to put him away.

"Mommy?" Penny calls from the kitchen. I step out of the laundry room, sliding the door shut behind me.

"Want to help me with the pancakes?" I ask. She drags a chair over to the counter and stands on it while I set out the ingredients.

Penny watches my hands as I cook, visibly relaxed without her father around. She and I will get by just fine without him here. And one day, if she behaves, maybe I'll let her count my pennies.

The William Seabrook
Guide to Parenting

Paul Lubaczewski

Before deciding to take writing seriously Paul had done many things, printer, caving, the SCA, Brew-master, punk singer, music critic etc. Since then he has appeared in numerous science fiction, and horror magazines and anthologies. Born in Philadelphia Pennsylvania, he moved to Appalachia in his 30s for the peace and adventure found there. Author of over 50 published stories, his debut novel "I Never Eat...Cheesesteak" will be in stores early in 2019

Andy looked at the clock above the TV, it told him what Andy didn't want to know, He would be home soon. He was always so infuriatingly punctual! Just once Andy would kill for him to be just a little bit late. But He never was, not since they had gotten here. Andy took it as his cue, it was time to find a save point and wrap up on the X-box for now. He didn't approve of it after He was home.

As if by clockwork, just as Andy was putting the controller back, the door opened and there He was, standing there holding a bag of groceries like he always did. He never wanted to buy more than enough groceries than what they would need for the next day for whatever reason. Andy didn't ask why, Andy didn't ask a lot of questions, it was just a bad idea.

"Honey I'm home!" He called out with a smile coming in the door and walking the bag of groceries to the kitchen.

That was the cue for everyone to line up for inspection. Andy, his twelve-year-old sister Tammy, and their little brother Timmy all in a row. Mother came out of her bedroom, where she had been lying down to rest. She needed to do that a lot now for some reason.

There was some clanking in the kitchen, as He put things away. All three of them shook a bit, worry eating at them as to what his mood might be tonight. They never could tell, some days it would be happiness and domestic bliss, but not every night. You just had to hope. Andy looked up and saw the same worry flooding his mother's face, try as she might, to conceal her fear of him.

When He came back out into the living room, Andy inwardly relaxed. He had his domestic expression on his face. As long as nobody screwed it up and made him mad, tonight would be just about bearable. He walked over to Andy's mother, and took her in his arms and kissed her.

"Busy day today dear?" she said as if someone had coached her.

He chuckled and said, "Oh boy, if you only knew. But, brought home some meat for dinner! I'll cook it up in just a minute!"

"That will make things easy," her voice betraying her lassitude.

"And how are the kids?" He said turning his attention to Andy and his siblings. His eyes seemed to linger on Tammy for some reason, before looking directly at Andy. For whatever reason, He had chosen Andy as the spokesman for the three of them, "So how was today, have fun and all?"

"Sure...Dad," Andy replied. This was probably why He focused on Andy, Andy was the last to call him Dad. Andy still had the bruises from his correction on that. HE could beat Andy into calling him dad out loud, but in Andy's mind, HE would always be Richard, or HE, nothing but. Andy didn't know where his Dad was, but it sure as hell wasn't Richard.

"Well, I brought you all a movie to watch while I make dinner. Then after dinner, it's off to bed so your Mom and I can watch something more adult! But, "Richard's" eyes focused hard on Tammy, "you're getting around that time my girl, growing every day. Maybe one day real soon you can stay up to watch an adult movie with me and your Mom, Tammy!"

Andy didn't know why his mother's eyes looked stricken at that. It sounded like one of the more normal things Richard had ever suggested, but judging from the look on her face, it couldn't have meant anything good. But then again, since they had come to this apartment, since Richard had declared himself their Dad, what good thing had happened?

Richard handed over a Blu-ray to Tammy and went off into the kitchen with their Mom trailing along behind him. Tammy did as she was told and turned the TV on and popped in the disc. It was some big Hollywood family movie that had comedians none of them were supposed to have known about, but they had caught glimpses of doing their real material at a friend's house at some point. It wasn't as good as going outside, but, they weren't allowed to anymore anyway, so it would just have to do.

Dinner was quiet, it usually was, what could any of them possibly have to talk about? They weren't allowed to go out anymore, where interesting things might happen. Richard tried to make small talk of course, but they could only manage to feign so much interest in his office talk. So instead they all quietly ate their meal, it was pork again, it seemed to be pork every night. Andy figured Richard must be getting a good deal on it from somewhere, nobody could like pork that much.

After dinner, Richard brought out three bowls of ice cream for them to eat while Andy's mother and Richard did the dishes. Andy wasn't going to have any tonight, he spooned it on to Tammy and Timmy's bowl. Neither of them complained about that much, Tammy raised her eyebrow at it, but Andy just said, "I'm not in the mood for ice cream is all." He would have liked some ice cream just fine, but he didn't trust it. His Mom and Richard never had any, and almost like clockwork, almost as soon as the ice cream was finished, it was time for bed. It had to be hours earlier than their normal bedtime, but no sooner would they finishing scraping the last of it from their bowls than all three of them would be yawning and rubbing their eyes. Not tonight, Andy had plans for tonight.

Just as it always happened, right after they finished their dessert, all three of them went to the bathroom to wash up for bed, and just like always, both of his siblings were exhausted. Andy made a point of rubbing at his own eyes, so he'd match them in appearance at least. When they were all ushered into bed, and kissed goodnight by their mother, he looked every bit as tired as his brother and sister.

But he wasn't at all, Andy's eyes flew open when he heard Richard lock the door. The door was odd, it locked outside the room, not inside, like the handle had been put in backward somehow. Richard, Andy was sure that it was Richard, made a point of locking it behind himself. Locking them in for the night. But not tonight, Andy had a plan, and one he had been working on for days.

He waited until he heard the gentle snores of his siblings coming from their own beds before carefully reaching under his mattress letting his questing hand dig around a bit until he found what he needed. A bobby pin, one of his mother's that he had stolen. Andy had carefully removed the little rubber head from it and bent it back. He'd practiced what he needed to do repeatedly, the lock on the door was a simple one, made for an interior of a newer house, all it would take would be a little fiddling to get it open. When his mother had been resting, he had practiced awfully hard at doing it quickly and quietly.

Still, he needed to wait. Andy knew that every night they weren't really watching a movie. Richard and his mother were doing something in their room, he needed to wait until he heard noises coming from next door. Andy knew this was all wrong, he didn't know where their Dad was, but he knew Richard wasn't their Dad, no matter how much he made them call him that. Not letting any of them leave this apartment, that certainly wasn't normal either. Something was really, really wrong, and if Andy could get out while his Mom and Richard did whatever they did in their room, maybe he could get help!

When he heard the bed springs begin to creak in the next room, that was his cue. Andy didn't know what they did in there, but it almost sounded like they were jumping around on the bed! He got up as quietly as he could and moved over to the door. Sticking the straight part of the bobby pin into the little hole in the knob, he moved it back and forth a bit until he found the right spot, a slight push and a twist and the doorknob turned easily!

The door thankfully had clearly been recently installed and swung open easily and most importantly, silently. Andy moved as quietly as possible, hovering his little body over each step. He froze in his footsteps at what he saw next, the door to his Mother's room was open a little! There was a light on in there! He paused for a moment, what if he got caught out of his room? What if they saw him?

It took Andy more than a moment to get his breathing under control, but once the pounding of his own lungs subsided in his ears he cocked his head towards the partially opened door. There were noises coming from inside, the bed was creaking more violently than he'd noticed from his own room. Richard was making muffled grunting sounds. When he heard what could only be a whimper of pain from his Mom, his own breath caught in his throat!

All thoughts of escape left him in an instant! He had to see what was happening! He had to see if he could help his Mom after all! Slowly and fearfully he crept towards the door. Andy leaned in carefully so not to disturb the door in any way and put his eye to the crack to peer inside.

He had to stifle a gasp from what he saw. Lying on her back, was his Mom, her face turned towards him, she wasn't wearing very much in the way of clothing, just stockings and a bra made of some lacy material that had been partially shoved askew. She looked in pain, her eyes closed.

But Richard, Richard was completely nude, and moving his hips at his Mom really hard! His head was in the pillow next to his Mom's head and he didn't see Andy at all! Richard's movements must have been what caused his Mom so much pain! Andy knew this was really bad, this looked like what he and Dad had that talk about a while ago, and it was only supposed to be Mommies and Daddies that did that together, not his Mom and Richard!

He turned his eyes to the side, hoping to stop seeing what was happening, which caused Andy's eyes to fall on something else entirely! A gun! It was lying only a foot or so away on a low cheap dresser by the door. Andy could almost reach it!

Andy turned back to his Mom, and his fury at the whole thing rose up unbidden! Richard had a gun, he was making his Mom do bad things with him! It was at that moment Andy's Mom's eyelids fluttered open! For a second her eyes got large as she caught sight of Andy, but then her hand stretched out languidly from where she suffered, and Andy saw her point with her finger in the direction of the gun as if directing him and giving him her blessing!

There it was, he could make Richard get off his Mom all right. Slowly scarcely able to breathe, Andy let his hand creep into the room. If he could get his hand on the gun, his Dad had taken him to the gun range to teach him how to handle one! Just a little more.... a little more.... he felt his hand tighten around the grip. He picked the gun up carefully, slowly, not to make a noise. His thumb flicked up the safety.

The room erupted with the explosive retort of the gun! Richard didn't just move, he actually jumped off Andy's Mom in his panic at the noise falling backward landing up against the wall! The man automatically scrambled to his feet staring in horror at his own gun now pointed at him, his rapidly shrinking manhood bobbing and exposed. Backing up more, his hands raised, he didn't stop until he felt his nude buttocks press into the smooth surface of the wall itself!

"Hey....kiddo.... buddy.... just, just put down the gun OK, and we can talk about it OK son?" Richard stammered his eyes wide with terror, his face a rictus attempt at a soothing smile.

The gun erupted again, but this time, it wasn't at the ceiling.

"You aren't my Dad Richard," Andy said quietly.

Bill Jensen was standing in the hall staring through the two-way mirror of the observation window when Jack found him. His former partner looked older than his years right now, Jack could understand it, this case was a hellscape any way you cut it. Lives ruined, blood everywhere.

Bill nodded to acknowledge him. Jack joined him looking through the mirror at the family huddled there eating a meal they had sent out for, for them. "You saw the dental report, right? It was the kid's father."

Bill grunted at that, replying in a gravelly voice, "Disgusting what happened."

"They haven't charged the kid, have they?"

Bill looked shocked at that, his face turning rapidly towards Jack showing off the deep shadows around his eyes from the lack of sleep this was causing, "You shitting me? Kid's a god damned hero!"

Jack nodded at that, "He sure is."

Bill kept talking as if Jack had said nothing, "Guy fucking kills his business partner, and kidnaps the poor guys family, rapes the wife, holds them kids all hostage, unbelievable. I woke up last night sweating from what we found when we raided the other house, finding what was left of the partner, Jesus who does that to a human body? I mean wasn't killing him enough, sicko has to hack the body apart?"

"You'll get no argument from me there, buddy," Jack said putting a soothing hand on Bill's shoulder, "so why we still have 'em in custody at all?"

"I need something from forensics from the apartment he had them in," Bill said flatly.

"What could you need that we don't already have?"

Before Bill could answer a young uniform officer came up to Bill and handed him a manila envelope. The Detective nodded to him and tore the paper to get to the information he needed, saying to the uniform, "Hold up, I might need you to go get something."

While Jack watched him, he could see his old friend's face go pale with shock. "What the hell is it Bill?" he demanded of him.

Bill coughed to clear his throat, turning to the uniformed officer, "Yeah, you kid, umm go get me the department headshrinker Soczewski!" When the officer had scurried off Bill turned to his friend as pale as a ghost, "See there were a lot of brown wrappers in the trash. But I thought it was weird, cause there ain't a butcher's shop anywhere near the place, or between the creep's company and there, so I had them tested. It wasn't no pig's blood on the wrappers, it was AB negative! You know how rare that is in humans Jack? You wanna guess the Dad's blood type?"

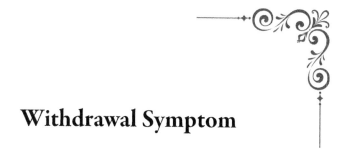

Withdrawal Symptom

Frank Roger

F rank Roger was born in 1957 in Ghent, Belgium. His first story appeared in 1975. By now he has a few hundred short stories to his credit, published in more than 40 languages. Apart from fiction, he also produces collages and visual art in a surrealist and satirical tradition.

White light suddenly flooded the small stage. All conversations died down as the audience craned their necks, so as not to miss a single detail.

A gorgeous blonde appeared, dressed in a dazzling red gown. She smiled and said:

"Good evening, ladies and gentlemen. You are about to witness one of the most spectacular performances ever brought to the stage. It will require total concentration from the Maestro, so please observe a respectful silence. I would also like to remind you that flash photography and video recording of this act are not allowed. When the show is finished, the house lights will come on and you will be asked to leave the theatre. Please don't come forward for autographs or a chat with the Maestro, as he will be exhausted and will retire quickly to recover from his efforts. Finally, I would like to point out that the Maestro will be naked all through this performance, for reasons that will be obvious soon. Now, ladies and gentlemen, are you ready?"

The audience replied with a unanimous "Yes". The blonde made a graceful gesture and said: "Please welcome... the Maestro."

The Maestro... so that was how uncle Frederick preferred to be called these days. Emma and I were eager to see his act, and looking forward to meeting him after the show. He knew we were attending, and had accepted to see us – for the first time in many years. We did not quite know what to expect, despite the few reviews we had read, which we had discarded as sheer sensationalism. Frederick had always played his own game, and according to his own rules. We would like to find out where that road had taken him now.

As the girl disappeared into the wings, an exceptionally slender man strode towards the centre of the stage, bathing in the spotlights and waiting until the applause had died down. He bowed, smiling, and then his face grew expressionless. We barely recognised Frederick, even if he had never been portly. How could he have lost so much weight?

Had he done that specifically for his shows? Had he jeopardised his health for his performances?

For a few moments, he just stood there, eyes closed, concentrating. The white glare of the spotlights glinted off his skin. He was stark naked, his head was clean-shaven, and all body hair had been removed as well. The audience watched in silence. Time went by, and nothing happened.

Then the Maestro opened his eyes and stared in front of him. He slowly lifted his right hand, put his fingers in his mouth and inhaled a few times, as if to gather strength. Then he shoved his hand deeper into his throat, swallowing with difficulty, as if he was on the verge of choking.

He managed to breathe normally and regularly, and remained unmoving for a few moments. The audience watched in stupefaction as the Maestro's lower arm disappeared completely into his throat in one smooth move.

A few cries rose from the front rows, and two women covered their eyes. The spectacle simply was too much for them.

As the silence was restored, the Maestro continued, slowly but steadily and methodically. It was now obvious he had performed this act countless times and had honed his technique to perfection. He inhaled deeply, opened his mouth until his lips seemed about to be torn apart and sucked in his arm almost to the shoulder.

Again he appeared to be choking, but quickly regained control. Did he really experience difficulties, or was he merely pretending to suffer problems so as to add drama to his performance?

A few women in the front rows left their seats and made their way to the exit. They could not take it any longer. Their departure did not seem to deter the Maestro. Perhaps he was not even paying attention to what happened in the theatre and concentrated exclusively on his act.

Sweat broke out all over his body, glistening in the spotlights. Was he now about to tackle the really hard part of the show?

A sudden spasm ran through his body, and his shoulder partly disappeared into his mouth, now stretched wide open, his lips reduced to two thin red lines on his face. His head was swollen, deformed with the effort of swallowing his own limb, even if it was a slender one. His kept his eyes closed, and his breathing grew increasingly laborious. How much further could he take this amazing feat?

Sweating profusely, his body shook with convulsions as he started to pull in his upper torso. The audience could not believe their eyes. Was this really happening? Was this an optical illusion, were they hallucinating? However, everyone felt that what they were watching was real, however surrealistic it appeared.

With a series of shuddering movements, his chest was tucked inside inch by inch. At this point the Maestro seemed to collapse; a few moments later the audience understood he had simply sunk to his knees, as his awkward position and his "incomplete" body no longer allowed him to stand upright.

He lowered himself further to a crouch, and used his left arm, still dangling from a corner of his mouth, to grab his right foot and hold up his leg, as if he wished to inspect it and check whether it was suitable for consumption.

To the audience's disbelief, he pushed his toes into his mouth and started inhaling deeply and swallowing. Judging from the sounds he produced and the spasms that shook his body, this was a particularly excruciating part of the performance. At some point, the convulsions and smothered screams became so alarming that a number of people assumed that things were going horrendously wrong, cried out in despair and even left the theatre in disgust.

Those who remained in their seats – about half of the original audience – quickly discovered that their fellow spectators need not have worried. The Maestro was making progress, even if he was straining himself beyond the point of what a normal human could endure.

At this point, I exchanged glances with Emma. A few whispered questions and answers taught me we had been thinking along the same lines, as had perhaps the rest of the audience.

If the Maestro had indeed swallowed a large part of his body, then where had it gone to? Into his stomach? His intestines? His abdomen was still incredibly slim, whereas logically one would expect the man to look like an anaconda, in whose swollen body the swallowed prey is clearly showing. His arm and his torso had to be somewhere! He couldn't have devoured and digested it all!

When the leg had disappeared completely, the Maestro allowed himself a short pause, so as to recover his strength. He was now virtually reduced to a ball lying on the stage, ahead with part of a torso and one pair of limbs, like a horribly disfigured war victim. We all thought the show was over – how could the man possibly continue?

With a mixture of awe, fascination, and horror we saw how he started to gobble up and swallow his genitals. Cries of both jubilation and outrage rose from the audience, and while some cheered and applauded, others shook their fists and left the theatre in disgust, judging the man had gone too far and transcended the boundaries of good taste.

As it dawned on everyone that the Maestro intended to go all the way, whispering voices could be heard, breaking the silence. No doubt people asked their wives, husbands or friends if a man could indeed swallow himself whole, and what would happen with the swallowed body parts.

As soon as his penis and testicles had been dealt with, the Maestro started work on his other leg. We watched in disbelief as that part of his body disappeared down his throat as well. Surely this could not be true? Had we somehow been tricked into believing what we saw, had we been fooled, misled? Had we missed the moment where the swallowing act had segued into a typical magician's illusion?

For a few moments, nothing happened. The Maestro's head was lying on the stage, his neck contorted in an unnatural way. Sweat poured profusely from his face, his expression was one of searing pain, and he produced all sorts of uncontrollable grunts and smothered screams.

More members of the audience grew sick and left. Emma and I stayed in our seats, even if it was extremely tough for us as well.

The house lights did not yet come on; this could only mean the show was not over. Everyone waited for what would happen. Would there be a grand finale, a climax taking the audience by surprise?

After a particularly alarming convulsion, the Maestro produced a thunderous belch, one that made the stage tremble, and then he threw up his own body, a slimy mass of shivering limbs and body parts that unfolded like a flower made of flesh and blood. He lay sprawling on the boards, looking dishevelled and exhausted, which was not surprising considering the ordeal he had just been through. The Maestro somehow pulled himself together, rose to his feet and looked the audience triumphantly in the eyes. He managed to stand upright, even if on wobbly legs. Was all this part of his act, or was he really on the verge of collapsing?

He received a standing ovation, bowed, obviously with difficulty, as if he had strained his muscles and frayed his nerves beyond repair, and disappeared into the wings.

The house lights came on and the audience – the remaining few – left the theatre, discussing the show they had witnessed. Emma and I waited patiently in our seats. After a few minutes, the girl with the red dress reappeared and asked us to follow her. She took us backstage, served us drinks and told us to wait until the Maestro had recovered sufficiently.

About fifteen minutes later he turned up, greeted us as if we were a couple of fans who wanted an autograph and took a seat in front of us. He was still in very bad shape – his act was clearly wearing him down.

"Uncle Frederick," Emma started. "Your act was fabulous, but how do you pull it off? What happens with those swallowed body parts? It's a trick, right? An illusion? There are some who claim your throat is a doorway into another dimension, where your swallowed parts go to until you bring them back, pretending to throw them up. I suppose you're aware of all those crackpot theories."

"I'm sure you don't expect me to divulge my professional secrets," he replied with a rasping and tired voice. "Not even to relatives. Especially not to relatives. Let's not talk about this. But I must admit I like that idea of a gateway to another dimension inside me." He chuckled.

"It must be a tough way to make a living," I offered. "How long do you think you can go on like this?"

A violent fit of coughing virtually tore him apart. When his breathing was back to normal, he said: "I know what you mean. And you're right. It took me endless hours of rehearsals before I got this act right and could perform it on stage, and it's getting more difficult and more painful each time. My biggest fear is that one day I won't be able to throw up and will end up stuck in my own body."

"We're all stuck in our own bodies," Emma replied and laughed. Uncle Frederick didn't seem to appreciate her remark.

I wondered if he had been serious about his fear. Did he expect us to believe he really swallowed his own body parts and then threw them up again? Or was he simply putting up a show, saying the same things he told fans he sometimes met after a show? And why was he doing that, considering we were close relatives of his?

"I always felt the need to withdraw," he said. "I made a career out of that attitude."

It was true that Uncle Frederick had always been the black sheep of the family, a man who had never been at home anywhere, and acted accordingly. He had severed the ties with most of us a long time ago and had never felt the need to stay in touch, even occasionally. He had ended up a loner, withdrawn from his family, his few friends, from social life altogether. He claimed no one understood him – and apparently didn't feel the need to be.

We sometimes wondered what had happened with him, until Emma found out he was the mysterious Maestro, "the man who swallowed himself whole", and decided to get back in touch with him. She booked tickets for a show and arranged a meeting afterwards. To our surprise, he agreed, but probably wondered why we had gone to the trouble. I started wondering myself now too.

Another violent fit of coughing shook him apart. When it was over, he said: "Sometimes I feel as if there's still a part of me inside. Something that's stuck there. Seriously, the coughing gets worse, and it's not the common cold."

"Your health is suffering from your act," Emma said.

"Yes," he admitted. "But there's no other way. Withdrawing has become a way of life to me. And I'm committed to taking it to the end."

"What's that supposed to mean?" I asked.

"You'll find out," he simply said.

Another fit of coughing almost seemed to kill him. When he breathed normally again, he said:

"Thanks for coming. Tell everyone I'm doing just fine. That's all I can say. I realise this may be hard for you to swallow." He chuckled at the pun. "Goodbye."

With those words, he left. Uncle Frederick had chosen to withdraw once again. We hadn't learned much, and never would – never should have hoped to.

We went back home with the little news we had garnered.

A FEW WEEKS LATER EMMA showed me a news item she had found.

"It's about Uncle Frederick," she said. "The Maestro is missing after an extraordinary performance. His last show, I guess we should call it."

The article described in detail a show the Maestro had given in Helsinki. It had begun as usual: the Maestro had put his fingers into his mouth and had swallowed one body part after another, until only his head, his neck and a stump of his torso were still lying on the boards.

Instead of throwing up his body again, as usual, this time he had also swallowed his own head, in one big gulp, while howling with pain and shaking as if he were suffocating. Such a feat is of course quite impossible, even more so than the rest of his act. The audience applauded, delighted because they had seen a very convincing illusion, and waited for the Maestro to reappear from the wings triumphantly or something like that. By doing that, he would admit it had all been an illusion – something most people assumed, apart from the diehard fans who believed he actually swallowed himself.

But the Maestro did not reappear, nor did he throw up himself again. It was not clear where he had gone too. His assistant told the audience the show was over, and cancelled all following shows. The Maestro (the article didn't mention his real name – maybe we were the only ones who knew how he was called) was declared missing, and still is to this day.

The police investigated the matter, but couldn't find any clues. They're no longer working on the case.

I discussed it with Emma, and we think we understand. Uncle Frederick has withdrawn completely, even from the career he made from his "withdrawing attitude" as he called it. He finally went all the way, as he announced us that day. He has withdrawn from life itself now, not just from us or his fellow men or society.

We have no idea where he is now and don't expect to find out. Nor do we hope to discover the truth behind his final disappearing act. The mystery will remain.

Only his diehard fans are convinced he swallowed himself whole, and for one unfathomable reason could not or chose not to throw up himself again. They're still waiting for his return.

It doesn't really matter who's right. The bottom line is that Uncle Frederick has left us. He has withdrawn beyond the point of return. We can only hope he's happy now.

It's what we told the rest of our family. Needless to say, some of them found the story hard to swallow...

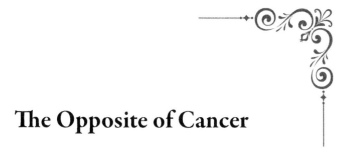

The Opposite of Cancer

J.F. Capps

J.F. Capps is currently 33 years old, but he's been writing since about age ten. He was composing stories through drawings and picture books of toys he posed before that. He started finding his own style as an author around age 16. He spent twelve years of his adult life with the Marine Corps, both active duty and reserve components, and currently works in corporate security management (which sounds much fancier than it is). He decided when he was 31 that it was time to start soliciting some of my work if he ever plans to make a career out of his passion instead of keeping it a hobby. He live in the hills of east Tennessee with his wife and four kids.

Tom had cancer.

He didn't know it at first. Two signs came together over a short period of time. His belly started to hurt. Tom never had a high tolerance for pain anyway, so the quick onset took him by storm. He ignored the dull ache in the beginning and went on to his job in IT with a stomach full of Tylenol and hope. He moved on to stronger stuff after the Tylenol stopped helping; hydromorphone, Oxy-8, that sort of thing, all of which he acquired through dealers that he met on the street in seedy situations he didn't want to be part of but found it necessary to partake in.

The second sign came at about the same time; the slow, dull yellow fading of his eyes. His vision didn't falter or flux, but the color change became noticeable to him when he looked in the mirror. This drove him to his computer, where he discovered the moniker of this symptom. Jaundice. There was a plethora of information on every 'mommy group' he could find on how to treat the malady, from carrot and spinach juices to sunlight, and he realized that the onset coincided with the number of hours he spent sitting on his ass in front of the new MMORPG that released a few weeks prior.

So Tom would sit at home taking his street bought pills, playing his game, ignoring his symptoms, and all the while telling himself that it was something easily explainable. He was overthinking it all. He began to spend more time than usual outside in the sun to counter the effects of jaundice but realized that wasn't working when his skin began to yellow and his eyes got worse. He blamed the waning of his appetite on the near-constant stomach pain coupled with the blatant abuse of the pills, and then the protrusion of his stomach on the swelling of his liver and the twenty plus pills he was eating a day.

Never having been a big man to begin with, Tom was little more than skin and bones when he passed out at work. His weight, what little he'd had, fell off him once he diminished to eating once a day. If he ate at all. One of his co-workers commented to him that his yellow pal-

lor had been replaced with a near gray look. Tom ignored this. He was
in more of a haze nowadays and, had it not been for fainting that day
he'd have been terminated from employment for being useless.

Tom awoke several days later in a room at a hospital surrounded by
instruments and gadgets and beeping devices with all manner of cords
and tubes and hoses running in and out of his body. He fainted again.
Tom had been diagnosed by his mother at the ripe old age of eight years
old as having iatrophobia, or, in laymen's terms, an acute fear of doctors.
That much was true. His was horrified, terrified, mortified of doctors.
He would have much rather charged through the gates of Hell with
nothing more than a bad attitude and his cock in his hand than to drive
past the doctor's office, let alone go in.

Deep down, Tom suspected that she preyed upon his childhood
fear of getting shots to keep from having to put in the effort of taking
him, which had stoked the actual fires of a true phobia. It was that
much harder to sit and listen to what the doctors came in to tell him
later, once he came to accept the feeding tube in his nose and down his
throat, or the myriad of IVs in either arm, or the catheter (holy shit the
catheter) that was leaking piss out of his body into a nifty little bag on
the side of the bed. Or how about the half dozen electrode patches all
over his body that itched like hell?

Then they told him he had cancer.

And then Tom panicked. So they sedated him. And he panicked
again when he woke up. He didn't know when he entered the hospital
or what day it was now, but he craved a fix. The sedative was a nice little
reminder of what his life was before he'd passed out at work, but it also
reawakened that need, that drive for the pills.

When the doctors came back they explained his situation to him,
which was more dire than a simple diagnosis of cancer. He had developed pancreatic cancer which had advanced to a point where there
were no conventional treatment options left. It had spread to his liver,
lungs, and some of his ribs. The doctors removed most of his ribs, most-

ly those on the left side of his body, and the lower quarter of his left lung. They couldn't do radiation or chemotherapy treatments because of the cancer in his liver, so they removed what they could during the intensive surgery, but all that was left now, aside from more surgeries and monitoring, was to try immunotherapy.

"We have a particular treatment plan in mind, Thomas." One of the doctors, a woman named Voiles, said. "Do you understand what cancer is?"

"Tom." He said. She smiled as she sat on the side of his bed. His body shifted as her weight dipped the foam mattress.

"Tom." She said. "Do you understand what cancer is?"

"No."

"Cancer is when the gene that inhibits the growth of your cells gets turned off, usually by a chemical influence, and then those cells begin to grow out of control. Does that make sense?"

Tom nodded.

"The treatment we have in mind corrects this gene in the afflicted area with help of a technology called CRISPR. Have you heard of it?"

Tom nodded again.

"I could try to break down the exact science of how this process works all day, but I really think you'd be better served if I summarize." Doctor Voiles said. One of her colleagues was across from her at a wash station in the corner of the room. He was leaned back, a tablet in one hand, peering over the top of his glasses at the two of them. A stylus was suspended between two fingers. She went on. "We create a batch of stem cells here in a lab using a strand of your own DNA that we have modified with CRISPR. In that original strand of DNA, we modify the gene that allows for such aggressive cell division. Then, we introduce these cells back into your body, right where the damage started. In your case, it'll be the pancreas, liver, lungs, as well as your ribs. Following me so far?"

Tom's face was stretched downwards into a perpetual look of dumbness. He felt the residual shock and detachment to the entire ordeal. Dr. Voiles waved a hand over his face when he didn't respond.

"Wuh, what?" He said, snapping back to reality. "Oh, yes, yes, I think I follow."

She patted his knee, then continued. Dr. Voiles was a competent, talented, physician, but she wasn't good at sugar coating things or expressing outward sympathy, even when she felt bad for someone, such as Tom Strickland before her.

"Ok, good." She said, removing her hand from his knee. "Once we place these new cells inside you they should start dividing in the afflicted organs and replace the cells that are so aggressively dividing now that are causing your cancer.

Because of the modifications we have made they should work to replace the afflicted cells with these newer, stable cells, and then we can work it out from there. We may be able to regrow the damaged and removed portions of your ribs and organs as well, but I think the first thing's first is to stop the spread of the cancer and destroy it."

Tom wondered what 'work it out from there' meant. It was hard for him to accept everything that had happened, and when the man with the tablet walked over to him so that he could start the paperwork process he signed without reading. His head spun as he sunk back into his pillow, letting exhaustion crash into him, but sleep, he knew, wasn't coming.

"Can I have something to take the edge off?" Tom said. It was a genuine question. He didn't feel like he was craving the dope the way he used to, but he knew now that everything she had hit him with in the last few minutes had psychologically wrecked him. He remembered one in high school when a girl, he thought her name was Jennie, had started dating a guy that he hated. Of course, she hadn't known Tom existed, but it still didn't stop the overwhelming sense of hurt and resentment that her supposed betrayal brought on. It was like someone punched their hand through his abdominal wall and twisted his guts into knots. He didn't sleep for a week. Barely ate. Could do nothing but lay in his bed and languish until one day his father ran him out of his bed and made him do yard work to get over 'whatever girl-fueled stupor you're in', as the old man put it.

This, though...there was something worse about this. A girl who didn't know him hadn't betrayed him this time. His own body had.

"Sure thing." Dr. Voiles said with a smile. She rose to join the fellow with the clipboard. After she left a nurse came in with a little white pill and placed it under his tongue. He was asleep within minutes.

TOM'S SLEEP WAS SO fitful and full of nightmares he couldn't escape because he had asked to be sedated. He was trapped in his own head with his cancer, watching as it morphed him, changed him into a monster. His legs ceased working, and he dragged himself along on the ground, his belly getting shredded over the rough surface of concrete and asphalt and raked deep with the gravel that was often found there. He felt the burning grit dig into cuts it left along his skin.

His side bulged. He could feel the burning pressure of the tumor gestating inside him as it pushed his other, healthy organs aside to make room for itself. His ribs were pulsing outward, cracking, groaning with the pressure exerted on them, before they began to break one by one. Some emerged from the skin and muscle of his side. Tom wanted to scream as the cancer continued to spread until its mass was too big to be contained any longer within his torso and a bulbous, veiny growth started to protrude from his side. It expanded at an exponential rate, the bag of raw flesh, membranous sinew, and blood gorged veins growing to the size of a tennis ball, a volleyball, a basketball, and then on to sizes harder for Tom to describe in his state of lucid sleep. A turkey. A large, overstuffed trash bag. It started to droop toward the floor then.

Panic seized him. The pressure of his tumor was putting so much strain on his diaphragm and lungs that he couldn't breathe. Worse, still, he could feel his heart slowing. He was dying. The panicked worry about the enormous herniation of his side was replaced now by his body's need for oxygen, nutrients, life-sustaining chemicals all brought to the various limbs and organs by the flow of blood. He was dying, though he couldn't tell if it was in the dream or if it was reality and he was going to be aware of the entire process but unable to do anything about it. He couldn't wake up. Couldn't panic save to think about what was happening. Couldn't cry out for help, to alert the hospital staff of what was happening.

His throat was closing. Oh dear God, his throat was closing! However bad the feeling of imminent asphyxiation was when the tumor ceased the function of his diaphragm was nothing, nothing, compared to the crawling pressure that was coming up his esophagus, past the epiglottis, forcing that valve closed, and then into his throat.

He was floating above his body now as all these sensations intensified, amplified to maddening levels that no sane man could take. He looked down upon himself, upon his eyes, forced closed by the sedative. He could see himself struggling for air, could see the tumor that was the size of a car spreading across the room, no, across its own hospital bed and then across the room. He could see the way his neck was growing, expanding into something new. Not a neck anymore but more of a ball that his head was mounted upon. Still growing. Pulsing. Beating.

His mouth opened. His tongue lolled out. Then, following behind it, was his heart, pressing up and out of his body as one rhythmically contracting horror, freed from the strain of the cancer to function now that it was removed from its rightful place.

There was a groan, though nothing emanated by human vocal cords. It was something else, something Tom was having trouble placing. He watched his heart slip over the left side of the bed and descend toward the floor, tethered to him by the aorta or, perhaps, the superior vena cava. Or inferior vena cava. Or whatever the hell it was. He was no anatomist.

He realized that the groan wasn't a human sound at all. Not in a sense, at least. It was coming from inside his chest, which was now heaved up into the air like a barrel. He'd always dreamed of having a nice chest with which to impress the ladies. But this...this...

It exploded, his sternum rupturing upward and outward, sheering through the skin. His lungs, now able to work with the pressure off them, started to inhale and exhale, the base of each blowing up and exiting the newly formed cavity before deflating and retreating into the meaty recess of his chest.

TOM WOKE UP.

He was still in the hospital.

The cool, stagnant, over sterilized air of the room pervaded all around him. He looked at the digital clock on the wall. He had been there for a week.

He was hungry. He picked up the remote call button and pressed it, sending a signal out of the room and to the nurse's station. A voice replied to him through the little device, and he requested food. His mouth salivated as he asked for it. He hadn't seen Dr. Voiles in a few days, but the last time he talked to her he admitted that he'd been suffering from a reduced appetite. Now his hunger returned more fervent than ever. The food they brought him was bland, but he tore into it, his plastic fork struggling to make any sort of work of the overcooked chicken breast before him so he picked it up in his hand and took a bite out of it.

One of his teeth wiggled.

Tom thought about this but refused to stop eating. It hadn't presented the same sensation to him that he felt as a kid when a tooth was loose; the alarming, almost painful feeling of the enameled molar or cuspid or whatever tearing itself free of his gums. This felt like shedding of dead tissue.

He continued to eat. He tasted blood at one point but signed it off as belonging to the area around the loosened tooth. He went to the bathroom when he was done to inspect his mouth and was disturbed to find that all his front teeth were loose. What's more, he was missing his top left incisor. He hadn't noticed it falling out. Had he swallowed it while eating?

Tom decided that it wasn't normal for his teeth to be falling out without reason, so he hit the call button again, and described his plight when the nurse replied. Dr. Voiles arrived less than fifteen minutes later, this time accompanied by two colleagues. She had Tom sit on the edge of his bed while she used one gloved hand to hold his mouth open and the other to manipulate his teeth with her finger. Most of them were loose. She exchanged medical talk with her guests that Tom didn't understand, and then smiled and told him in a calm, reassuring voice, that she was sure it was a side effect of the gene therapy and that she was also sure it could be fixed. One of the teeth popped out while she said this, and she bagged it in a glove and took it with her, explaining that she was going to have the lab run some tests.

Tom took his opportunity to nap again. He lay back and went to sleep. There were no dreams, no sensations whatsoever, just black oblivion from which he emerged still exhausted. Maybe more so than when he went to sleep.

He reached up to his face to scratch an itch. The nail on his right index finger flaked off, falling to the sheet with a streamer of germinal matrix trailing behind it. There was no pain, only the slight tugging sensation that culminated with the loss of the nail. He looked at his hand, and then realized that the nail on his middle finger was gone as well, replaced by a pustulent blister that hadn't been there when he went to sleep.

A cold, wet sensation was running down his face.

Tom got out of his bed and went to the nearest mirror, where he found the skin on his face was cracked open and bleeding, but the blood that was leaking from the wound lacked the healthy red he was so accustomed to. Instead, it was almost purple, or black; some darker shade that blood shouldn't be, even in the veins. He rolled up a tissue and pushed it against the ulcer, trying to stop the bleeding, but no matter how long he held pressure to it the blood continued to flow. It soaked the tissue through.

Tom was scared. First his teeth, now his face. He wasn't sure what was going on. He brought his free hand up and ran it through his hair and was shocked when handfuls of it came loose and rained down around him. He held the blood-soaked tissue to his face and looked, trying to discern what he was seeing, what was happening, before it dawned on him to check his bed. That's when he noticed the huge mat of hair left behind on his pillow. He flushed, heat washing over his body as he fought the urge to panic. He dropped his gown. Everywhere he looked his skin was flaking away, sloughing off his body like a molting reptile. Now his hands were shaking. He darted for the call button, hitting it for the third time that day.

"I need Dr. Voiles!" He said when the nurse answered. His voice cracked with panic. "I think there's something really wrong with me!"

The nurse hesitated. It sounded like there was frantic movement around the nurse's station.

"It's going to be just a moment, Mr. Strickland." The nurse said. Tom became aware of more noise outside his door. "Dr. Voiles is...uh...sick. We're calling a specialist up to see you."

He could tell she was struggling to keep her voice calm. Then he heard a hospital bed rolling and banging the wall in the next room.

He was surprised when he opened the door to find multiple nurses running up and down the halls, a quarter of them pushing hospital beds. They were all panicking, their actions matching the sounds of the nurse's station a moment before. Then there was a taser in his face.

"Step back inside your room, Mr. Strickland!" A man said, his voice muffled. Tom's eyes drifted with all the conviction he could muster, but things were beginning to grow very, very foggy for him. Not in the sense that he couldn't see, but more so in the sense that nothing he did see was making sense. He was stunned to see an armed police officer gloved up and wearing a gas mask leaning in close to him. Another was sprinting up the hall in their direction. "Step back inside your room now, Mr. Strickland, or I'll have no choice but to use force!"

He backed up, his naked form disappearing from their site behind the privacy curtain hanging inside the door. His own panic was setting in deeper. What was happening? He didn't understand why they were leaving him behind. He was a patient too!

The skin on the back of his left arm fell free, sticking to the floor with a wet slap. A trickle of blood followed. He could see the muscles in his arm moving as he lifted it up to examine what was going on.

"Is he still in there?" Someone said outside the door. Their voice was muffled, matching the cop's who threatened him with violence. He backed away from the curtain and realized that the floor was wet. He looked down. He was leaving bloody footprints. The curtain parted. Six people entered the room in hazmat suits. "Mr. Strickland...are you ok?"

They stopped, watching him with both scientific curiosity and abject horror. One was pointing with a pen at the bloody footprints and shed tissue. Tom backed toward the bathroom door, but they didn't offer to follow.

"Where's Dr. Voiles?" Tom said. His foot worked its way over the entrance to the bathroom. "I don't feel so good. I really need to see my doctor."

"Dr. Voiles is very sick." A woman said, the one that had been pointing at the stuff on the floor. "Tom, you are very sick. We are here to help you, but you have to trust us. We need you to come over here..."

"What's wrong with Dr. Voiles?" He said, uninterested in cooperation until he had some answers. He glanced in the mirror as he looked around from the...the...whoever they were, to himself, to his options of locking himself in the bathroom. He pulled his hand free from the door facing to wipe sweat from his face and realized that he left the pads of his fingers behind, the shed tissue sticking to the metal. He realized that his eyes were now red, far removed from the jaundiced yellow that had started him on this journey.

"You're uh...the gene treatment you were given...has mutated in an unexpected way. It uh...your body has ceased mitosis, and your DNA is breaking down into a mutant nucleotide strand that is infiltrating the DNA of other living organisms and is causing rapid irreparable cellular damage..."

"What's wrong with Dr. Voiles!?" He said again, grabbing the door. His fingers, slick with blood and weeping bodily fluids, slipped free the first time, but the second time the raw pads of the digits gripped. "What does any of this have to do with Dr. Voiles!?"

His penis fell off in that moment, the meaty stub of his member slapping against the tile floor. He looked down at the jagged stump where the skin and blood vessels had detached, most of which was hanging free like it was torn versus succumbing to gravity. At least his scrotum was still attached he thought. He felt faint. He brought one hand up and let the bloodied pad of his now missing fingertips explore the stump of what he had lost. He felt sick. He wavered on his feet for a moment before regaining his composure, or what little was left of it, and traced his fingers up over his stomach. Something felt...wrong. His abdomen felt heavy. There was a noticeable bulge forming in his stomach, and it was soft to the touch. He could push it back in with his fingers.

One broke from the force he exerted on it, bending backward in the middle. He assumed he didn't feel anything because the nerve endings were starting to die.

"These nucleotides behave like a virus or...prion...Mr. Strickland." The woman said, easing forward with an outstretched hand. Tom's eyes settled on the trembling rubber glove. Her voice was calm, soothing, but her body language gave away that she was terrified. "They behave something like a rogue protein, but instead of breaking your DNA and such down to replicate themselves they first infiltrate it to rewrite your genetic code. Then they replicate and spread and...well, as you can imagine, all these replicating nucleotides reproduce themselves exponentially until, finally, you get this explosion of decaying DNA strands and complete lack of mitosis that is required to keep the body running while the usually innate bacteria in your system activate and you start to break down and..."

The longer she talked the more flustered she became until she was out of breath but still trying to explain his extraordinary circumstance. The semblance of control she displayed moments before was gone and she was babbling. She stopped. Tom felt his abdomen again, stroking the bulge of his stomach until it burst. Hot liquid poured over his hand and the end of his arm and could see a mixture of liquids erupting from him; blood, bile, digestive juices, feces, all speckled with tiny pieces of tissue. His intestines followed and fell to pieces as they did so. He panicked, screamed, fell to his knees as he scooped up what he could of his innards and crammed them back into the tiny hole in his abdominal cavity, but ribbons of gut slipped between his fingers and pooled around his knees on the floor of the bathroom.

The woman didn't offer to move any closer.

"I think it's time to seal the whole level off and get the hell out of here." One of her colleagues said. The other five people in hazmat suits hadn't bothered moving away from the door. "The risk of infection is greater than the chance of saving him at this point, and he's deteriorating so rapidly that we're not going to be able to extract any valuable data before he completely breaks down."

Tom wanted to scream, to yell that they couldn't leave him, that he needed help and he needed Dr. Voiles, but the woman was already rejoining her team. They looked at him, at his outstretched hand with cold calculation. Something glimmered from inside her helmet, though he couldn't tell if it was tears or sweat, but regardless she didn't make any attempt to move back in his direction.

The skin on his stomach was peeling away now, falling into the floor in great sheets to join the strips of abdominal muscle and piles of liquifying organs. The room was growing black.

"I think we need to bring Dr. Voiles and the lab tech here, to this floor. Centralize the infection in one location."

"I think it's too late. At least a few of the nucleotides are in the water supply simply from when she was scrubbing her hands. There's no containing it."

The bloody-brown viscous mess of fluid that escaped from Tom was now acting as a lubricant. His body was sliding down the wall where he fell from his knees. His ass raked along the floor leaving an unspooled stretch of skin and muscle as he died, his body sinking in on itself as he came to his final resting place there, on the bathroom floor.

Near Evil

Ryan Bowling

Ryan Bowling has been writing horror fiction since 2011 and has authored two full length novels, three short screenplays, and over fifty short stories. He is currently working on a short story collection of science fiction/horror and is outlining his third novel. While in college, he entered his first short story entitled, "Catnapped," in a writing contest and won.

Biting cold winds seeped through the plastic covered window cracks, swirling around the living room dwelling like a hunting serpent bent on conquest. Steve Williams sat across his wife Brenda, of six months, on a sunken, beat-up couch. Steam rose from two cups of coffee on an oval-shaped table before them. Steve gazed at the steam rising from his cup, contemplating as to whether to take a sip or not. His leather jacket, lined with fur, did just enough to keep him warm. Brenda rocked back and forth, wearing her brown fur coat with her arms folded.

They said it would be days like this. Days that would challenge Steve's level of commitment to marriage. But he had no way of knowing that he would lose his job as a cable installer due to some corporate nonsense. Had to downsize, they told him. He wasn't a part of the elite. He wasn't good enough to be considered as a viable asset worth keeping. So they clipped him. He became just another serf slave to whose services were no longer needed.

"I'm... I'm so sorry. I really am. It's not my fault, you believe that don't you?" A painful lump formed in Steve's throat. Brenda didn't say one word. Her hands cupped in her lap, and staring down, she continued to rock back and forth in silence. "I couldn't control what happened," Steve said. "You have to believe that. You know they don't care about human life. They only care about profits, nothing more. You know that."

Brenda suddenly raised her head and gazed at Steve with piercing eyes. "You could have talked to them. You could've said something. Anything to keep your job. But you didn't. Now we can't pay the bills and I'm three months pregnant. Did you forget about that?" She shivered from the bitter cold as her eyes teared up.

Steve stooped down before her and held her hands. He rubbed his lips as he struggled to get the right words out. What could he say to her? She was suffering.

Sitting in a cold apartment because he couldn't hold a job. "Honey, you. . ." he choked, and forced himself to look away. He was failing as a man and he knew it. The predictions of Brenda's mother was coming true. "Do you believe me anymore," he said, staring into Brenda's eyes. "Do you? Huh? I'm trying. I'm really trying."

Brenda unfolded her hands and placed them both on Steve's hands. "I'm sorry about the way I reacted. But I'm worried right now. We don't have any heat, food is low, and you haven't found work in a while. How do you expect me to feel? For God sakes, I'm pregnant, baby. I'm getting tired. Really tired."

Choked with helplessness, Steve ran into the bathroom and slammed the door. He leaned against the wall with his hands over his mouth as warm tears flowed. What could he say? That everything would be alright? He said that already, but nothing changed. Oh, yea, they said he had to be positive. But he was being positive. Being positive didn't change his wife's attitude. It didn't change his unemployment situation. And it certainly didn't change. . .

Wait a minute. He pulled his wallet out of his back pocket and discovered his master card still had some cash available. Just enough to buy some groceries for at least a few days. Hopefully, this would settle the tension between him and Brenda. Food tends to do that. He left the bathroom and stood near the exit hallway door. "You want something to eat?" he said. "I got a little money left on my credit card and I was wondering if. . ."

"Yes, I do," Brenda said, still rocking back and forth.

Steve let out a breath of relief and opened the door to the hallway. Warm air rushed past him, contrasting the frigid air in his apartment. He plopped his forehead on the door and clenched his fists together so hard, his knuckles throbbed.

Lord, please let this work, he thought. "You can do this," he whispered. "You are a man! You hear me? You are a man!" He slowly turned around and nearly lost his balance at a lumbering figure standing several feet before him.

Mr. Gus Howard Vant, a six feet ten inch giant of a man with long flowing dark hair, wearing a black leather jacket, had his back turned away from Steve as he locked his door. He stood at his door for an unusually long time, fiddling with the lock mechanism as if he didn't know what to do. With unhurried ease, he turned around and stared with full stance, not saying a single word.

"Ah, hello... I mean, how are you, sir?" Steve's attention immediately shifted from his wife to this human monster whose shadow filled the space where he stood. Gus stared for several seconds, then trudged down the hallway and onto the elevator. Steve hardly saw the man except on certain occasions when he'd leave his apartment.

Having been taught proper manners, Steve introduced himself on his first day of neighborly kindness, which was around three months ago. Gus obviously was a very busy man, because he was constantly on the go. Always in and out of his apartment.

"Excuse me, is anybody out there?" A muffled voice echoed through Gus's door.

Steve trembled in his shoes as he locked his eyes in that direction. "Yea, uh, yes. Are you alright?"

"Oh, yea, I'm just fine. I just... I just wanted to know if you had a cup of water?"

Steve paused for a second, somewhat put off at this person's question. What, they didn't have any water in their own apartment? "Okay, well hold on for a minute and I'll get you a cup." He unlocked his door and stepped inside.

"Wow, that was quick," Brenda said, hugging her midsection with her back still turned.

Steve walked into the kitchen and grabbed a drinking glass from the drainer. "Nah, not yet," he said, while water poured into the glass from the faucet. "You know that guy, ah, what's his name... Oh yea,

Gus, well someone, I don't know who, wants some water out of his apartment."

"What's wrong with that?" Brenda said.

"Nothing I guess. It's just that they didn't open their door. I don't even know how the person looks." Steve sauntered over to the couch where Brenda sat. "You're not still mad at me are you?"

Brenda let out a slight chuckle. "Of course not." She puckered her lips and closed her eyes. Steve placed one of his love taps right in the center.

He was thrilled to know that he could leave on a high note. Brenda was good for that. Being angry one moment and happy the next. "I love you," he said, staring into her eyes as if they'd just gotten married. Brenda returned the compliment with equal emotion.

Steve walked outside and locked his door, confident that he'd be back with good news. "I have some water. You still want it?" He inched his way over to Gus's door, waiting for an answer.

A full ten seconds went by before the person spoke. "Oh thank you so much. I'm really, really thirsty. Thank you so much. Could you put it like... on the floor? You know, like, I'll grab it from the bottom."

Steve gasped. Put it on the floor? He thought. "Alrighty then. If that's what you want." He placed the glass on the floor several inches away so it could be reached. "By the way, you can keep the glass. I won't be needing it anymore."

Ten seconds went by before the door opened about six inches. Steve was taken back by a bony hand which reached out to snatch the glass of water. And a most repulsive stench seeped into the hallway from that apartment. He never smelled a dead body. Never even came near one. But he could only imagine. Dear God, he could only imagine. The door shut and all he could hear was terrible gulping sounds. As if whoever was in there, hadn't drunk water in days. He walked away and entered the elevator further down the hall. Who was that person? He thought. Was Gus abusing his wife? Or girlfriend? Or maybe his child?

And God, that smell. That stench. How in the world could he live in that?

He exited the elevator on the first floor and left the building. A stream of biting cold air hit him as he rushed to his blue Nissan and stepped in. As he started the car, he noticed Gus driving up and parking his black Toyota towards the end of the lot. He turned his vehicle off and just sat lifeless, with his hands gripping the steering wheel. Steve could've just driven off, but somehow he was compelled to see what Gus would do.

"Let me get out of here," Steve said. As he pulled off he saw Gus leave his car with two large, black garbage bags in both hands. Something chilled Steve about the bags. They were just garbage bags. But something just wasn't right about the way they were shaped. They were deformed. As if thick rods were sticking out of the sides. Thoroughly creeped out, Steve drove off and onto Superior Avenue, headed towards Save A Lot grocery store. A small picture of his wife hung on the sun visor. Her hair and face decked out, it made his journey a lot easier.

He drove on a snow-covered street, using the most extreme caution as he swirled in and out of ice spots, trying to avoid hitting passing vehicles. By the time he'd arrived at the grocery store, half an hour had passed by.

He parked his car near the entrance and stepped out into the bitter cold. Barely able to breathe, he walked through the doors and was shocked at how many people were out shopping. Without a doubt, he'd be there for a while. He grabbed a shopping cart and strolled down the frozen meats section contemplating what to pick up when his cell phone vibrated in his pocket. Startled by its suddenness, he pulled his phone out and gazed into the screen. It was a private number. Odd, considering the fact that he never hardly received private calls. Ignoring the call, he continued on his shopping journey.

But as he walked further down several sections, his phone rang again. Frustrated, he snatched it out of his pocket and stared into the screen. Another private number. This time, he answered. "Hello? Who is it?" All he could hear was heavy breathing, like someone having an asthma attack. "Look, I don't have time for games. Whoever this is, you better answer or. . ."

"I see you." A deep, monotone voice permeated the phone.

With rapid haste, Steve looked around, his heart pounding. "I'm hanging up," he said. "Have a nice. . ."

"She's very, very, very, very, very, prettyyyyyyy."

Steve jammed the phone back into his pocket and raced towards an empty line. Who was 'she?' he thought. He could feel the phone vibrating in his pocket. Taunting him. Edging him to answer.

As he raced towards an available line, every face, every expression, became the potential torturer. They all seemed to be grinning at him. Mocking his incompetence. Their twisted faces flashing pass him like pictures in a projector. Someone in this line was calling him on his phone. He just knew it. Oh, they look away, acting like they don't see him. But he knew. He knew.

He reached a line and stood behind an old lady with a cart full. All the other lines were much worse and he had no other choice. Every step closer to the cashier felt like a fraction of an inch. The phone buzzed in his pocket constantly, poking his leg with its tormenting ways. Tiny beads of sweat peaked on his forehead, prompting him to snatch the phone out of his pocket. He stared at the screen and discovered it was a text message.

She tastes so good. Her skin. Her face. Her eyes. A smiley face popped up beside the text. Steve jammed the phone back in his pocket. After a torturous fifteen minutes of waiting, he finally paid for his food and literally ran out of the store.

Oh God, don't let this be my wife, he thought. He opened his car door, threw the bag of groceries in back, and turned the ignition. After a series of sputters, the car started and he sped out onto Superior Avenue. His car slid several times before he was able to gain control again.

Hands trembling on the steering wheel, his phone vibrated in his pocket again and again. Resisting the temptation to ignore, he pulled his phone out and stared into the screen.

I think you better hurry up. I don't think she is gonna' make it. The pain is beyond comprehension. I think you better hurry, please.

Steve slammed his phone on the passenger seat. "It's my wife! It's my... wife." He continuously slammed his hand on the steering wheel, screaming at the top of his lungs. "You better not harm my wife you bastard! Whoever you are, you better not harm her."

He pulled up into the parking lot, nearly hitting several cars as he shut his off and opened the door, leaving the groceries behind. A blanket of snow came out of nowhere, blinding him on his way to the front door entrance. He entered using his keycard and stepped on the elevator to the fourth floor. His heart raced so fast, he thought he would have a heart attack.

The elevator door opened and he ran towards his apartment which was at the very end. His hands shaking, he took out his key to unlock the door, and that's when his heart literally stopped beating.

The door was already unlocked.

Standing open several inches, It beckoned him to enter. Frigid air smashed into his face like an unwelcome guest hiding behind a veil. He knew he locked it when he left. Did Brenda leave and forget to lock it? He wasn't sure. A new level of fear overshadowed him as he gently pushed the door open. "Brenda, are you okay in there?" He stood totally still in the doorway, hoping beyond all hope she'd answer. But the living room was empty of any signs. She wasn't on the sofa. She wasn't on any of the chairs. Nothing.

She's in the bathroom, he thought. Where else would she be? He turned and entered the bathroom on his right, but no Brenda. Not even a trace of her perfume. He pressed his hands into tight fists, cracking his knuckles. His throat dried up into a sand dune as he hacked out words in short bursts.

The phone rang in his pocket and he answered without hesitation. "Who... who... who is it?" He bit down on his bottom lip, drawing blood.

"If you want to know," the voice said, "then you need to step out of that apartment of yours, or else this whore will die."

Steve shoved the phone back in his pocket and stepped out into the hallway. He stood facing Gus Vant's door, not knowing who this person was or where he was. Then a revelation materialized before him. Gus's door crept open about a foot, spilling out putrid rot beyond anything Steve ever smelled. Something like a mixture of stale urine, vomit, and decaying flesh.

"Get in here boy."

It was Gus's voice, coming from somewhere in the apartment. Steve couldn't tell where, but he knew he had to enter. Covering his mouth with one hand, he pushed the door open and walked in. He stood facing the door, not wanting to look behind him.

"Turn around boy." Gus's disembodied voice echoed across the room. "I said turn around!" he screamed.

Steve shut his eyes for a second, taking in deep, harsh breaths. He slowly turned around. What he saw put his heart into overdrive. To his left, ten feet away, was a closet with a sliding door wide open. On the outside, stood a monstrosity of pain and horror.

The person, who turned out to be a male, whom he gave a glass of water to earlier, was standing completely nude with dog chains around his neck, arms, and feet, which was clamped to a large spike inside the closet. His body was covered from head to toe with hundreds of three-inch blood-soaked gashes. His dark hair was matted to knots that looked like strips of raw flesh. A half eaten can of dog food laid at his feet.

In total shock, Steve backed himself into the door, shutting it close. He slapped his hands over his face, not believing what he was seeing. "I'm thirsty! I'm so thirsty!" the mangled man kept saying. But Steve couldn't pull himself to look upon such a nightmare. He wanted his wife. He wanted Brenda.

Muffled noises made him move his hands from his eyes. But he wished he had kept them closed. Because nothing could prepare him for what he saw in that place called a living room. Something even hell wouldn't vomit up, surrounded him. All around him, the black painted walls were draped with dozens of bloody human faces hanging from nails. Vacant, dark holes where their eyes used to be, gazed back at Steve. Their mouths, screaming for help that would never come, stood wide open.

Gus stood in back of Brenda with an extension cord with part of the cord exposed at the end and plugged into the wall behind him. Brenda sat on a metal chair stripped naked and covered in clear plastic from her torso to the top of her neck. Her bare feet were in a bucket of water and her hands were tied behind her back with ropes. Her bleeding, lacerated face portrayed a look of encroaching death.

Leaking with stale grease, the kitchen stove sat in a corner near a round table filled with empty picture frames with name tags at the bottoms. Two men were sitting on chairs across from Gus and Brenda, covered in plastic from their feet to their neck. Various tools of demise laid on the floor next to the chairs. A hacksaw. Screwdriver. Butcher knife. In all four corners of the living room, were horribly butchered corpses neatly stacked to the ceiling and covered in clear plastic.

His stomach heaving, Steve bent over and vomited.

Gus walked over to the door, locked it, then stood in front of the two men sitting on the chairs. Steve wiped his mouth, struggling to stand up. "What... what do you want?" he said, leaning against the wall. Gus said nothing. He merely walked over to a radio sitting on the table and turned the channel to an oldies station.

It was playing the end theme song to the movie "The Shining," entitled "Midnight, the stars and you." It filled the atmosphere with a soothing yet out of place tone that sent chills up Steve's spine.

Gus slowly turned around to face Steve. His enormous form, towering over the two men. He gazed upon Steve with an intensity beyond understanding.

It was as if his eyes were shooting invisible rays of pulsating agony. Without answering, he turned back around, grabbed the hacksaw, and stood in back of one of the men. He placed the tip of the hacksaw on his head, moving it back and forth without cutting into flesh.

Steve's heart pounded at Gus's look of gleeful amusement as he suddenly switched the hacksaw to the man's neck and began carving into soft flesh, slicing through tendons and muscles as if he was cutting a piece of bread, his bottom lip contorting to the music playing on the radio. Gurgling sounds followed as bright red blood gushed out until his head popped off with the demented ease of merely removing a lampshade. "I like how that feels," Gus said, tossing the severed head aside. "The smooth way in which the blade cuts into flesh. The sweet sounds of gurgling." He licked his fingers with his eyes slightly closed. "It's so beautiful."

Steve gritted his teeth, pulling every ounce of strength in him not to overreact. His heart raced, but he kept calm. "Please, please, let my wife go. Please. I won't tell anybody. I promise."

"That doesn't matter," Gus said, dropping the hacksaw and picking up the butcher knife. "That doesn't matter at all. And do you want to know why it doesn't matter?" He placed the tip of the knife on the other man's stomach. "It doesn't matter, because there is no one... on this floor... left."

With sickening ease, he rammed the entire blade into the man's gut, twisted it around like a corkscrew, then sliced downward.

The man bellowed out a horrible shriek as an avalanche of blood and innards splattered the floor. Gus spewed a hauntingly deranged laugh, filling the living room with a pervasive evil that escaped human capacity. "You like what you see?" he said, dropping the knife. "Because

I like what I see. I like it a lot. I have special plans for these pets. Very, special plans."

Tingling sensations shot up Steve's legs as he fought to stand high. With an agonizingly slow pace, Gus snatched the screwdriver and stood behind the other man, whose face was soaked in sweat. "Watch this," he said. He raised the screwdriver high, blinked at Steve, and began plunging the point into the man's chest and stomach, sending splats of blood through the air. Steve coughed up traces of spit, as he witnessed this man, this living creature, practically disembowel his victim with a screwdriver.

The man's intestines bubbled out as Gus tirelessly stabbed away. "I love it!" he screamed. "I love it!" It seemed there was no limit to his rage. He slashed away at the man's throat, arms, stomach, eyes, and face in a mad fury until nothing remained but a lump of blood-drenched meat. One eyeball hung from its socket like a displaced ornament. He dropped the screwdriver and grabbed the exposed extension cord.

Steve attempted to lunge forward, but Gus quickly intercepted and stood behind Brenda with the exposed cord hanging over the bucket of water. "Come any closer and I'll fry this whore," he said. "I have good plans for this pet." He repeatedly raised the extension cord up and down above the bucket, pulling Brenda's head back with his free hand at the same time.

Steve's head nearly burst open from an intense, probing headache as he gazed upon his wife, totally helpless. Her mouth gaped open and dripping with vomit. "Look... you don't have to do this. You don't have. . ."

Gus dipped the exposed wire into the bucket of water, sending Brenda on a frantic, body stiffening series of teeth grinding convulsions. She spewed foam and her toes and hands curled into a tight clench as urine poured onto the floor.

Heartbeat thrashing in his ears, Steve ran towards the lamp and lunged it at Gus's head, striking him in the center and knocking him onto the floor. Grabbing the opportunity, Steve jumped on Gus's chest and began squeezing his bulging throat. Every ounce of sour rage coursed through him as he tightened his grip, laughing at this beast of a man lying before him. He relished the pain he caused, as Gus's body went limp. Steve jumped up and shuffled over to Brenda, who was now semi-conscious.

"Come on baby, wake up. Wake up," he screamed, tearing the plastic off of her neck and torso. He shivered at the sight of the stacked corpses lying in all four corners. Then it dawned on him. Those corpses were the residents of the building. The entire floor was in this apartment.

As Steve tore the rest of the plastic off Brenda's face, something caught his attention, making him stop mid-stride. It was coming from one of the bedrooms down a hallway. It sounded like low moans that rose every few seconds, then went back down to a grim sob. Like someone crying behind one of the closed doors.

He'd been through enough. But he couldn't ignore what might be more victims. Seeing that Gus was unconscious, and knowing Brenda wasn't in any immediate danger, he crept over to one of the doors and placed his ear on the surface.

An old song from the rock group, Pink Floyd came over the radio entitled, "Another Brick in the Wall." Its ethereal lyrics seemed to dance in mid-air down the hallway, mixing with agonizing moans coming from behind the bedroom door. "Its... it's going to be alright. I'm going to get you out of there," Steve said.

He grabbed the knob, but just as he was about to open the door, what at first appeared to be one voice, became dozens of unrecognizable voices clashing against each other for space. Steve couldn't make out what they were trying to say. But whatever they were trying to say, he knew that if he didn't enter, they would die. Looking behind him once again, he opened the door and stared into the face of hell itself.

Dozens of nude men and women were chained to the walls and linked together by four-inch spikes sticking up from the floor. Steve gagged at the sight of layers of human entrails, scattered throughout the floor in a grizzly, vomit-inducing display of blood. Swirling dizziness attacked him, but he held onto the edge of the door, fighting his pulsing heart from exploding. He gazed upon severed arms poking their fingers up from beneath the viscera as if mocking him. Another old song played over the radio. It was Pink Floyd's "Breathe in the Air." It's sound echoed through the hallway and into the bedroom, as the chained victims moaned for relief.

Then something dripped onto Steve's head. Breathing heavily, he looked up and the muscles in his face immediately stiffened. It wasn't a normal ceiling. Positioned between the ceiling joists, were at least ten ravaged bodies hanging on hooks from the skin of their backs. There were hooks in their feet, legs, buttocks, and neck, and their stomachs were sliced open, revealing empty, blood caked spaces. They'd been completely gutted. Their eye sockets, empty and black as the pits of hell. Their puffy tongues hung from their mouths like skinless serpents.

Steve fell to the floor, trying desperately to hold himself up with one hand. The living victims screamed in unison, yanking on their chains. Before Steve could stand back up, Gus was behind him, brandishing a large chainsaw. He swept the sharp blade pass Steve's head, missing by inches. Steve rushed pass Gus, but missed the doorway, ramming himself into the wall. Shaking dizziness off, he turned around just in time to see a bloodbath take place before his eyes.

Gus ran over to one of the writhing victims, and with effortless motion, cut the man's head completely off. Blood spewed from the stump as Gus pursued his mad death chase, cutting off arms, legs, and heads, from the others, in a continuous blood-drenched frenzy, screaming to the top of his lungs. An old seventies song from the rock group Boston, entitled, "More than a feeling," blasted over the radio coming from the living room, clashing with screaming and the riveting sounds of the chainsaw carving into quivering flesh.

Limbs were tossed in the air by the swinging chainsaw blade as Gus went from victim to victim, sawing bodies in two, as steaming innards splattered the already gore-soaked floor in a monstrous heap of carnage. Seeing Gus's death obsession, Steve ran out of the bedroom, ripped the remaining plastic from Brenda's limp body, and headed towards the door. Before he could reach for the knob, Gus was on top of him, punching him in the back of his head. Smashing pain caused him to instantly release Brenda.

He swirled around and began slamming his fists into Gus's face with every ounce of strength left. His arms raged with fiery pain and fatigue the more he pounded this evil man. The chainsaw was gone, and for a second Steve felt that Gus wanted to torment him with his bare hands. He stood there, talking every blow Steve had to offer without flinching. Now was the time. He couldn't delay.

If he wanted to take Gus out, he would have to do something he never thought he would. Kill. He darted off, picked up the butcher knife used earlier off the floor, and lunged at Gus's bare throat. The entire blade sunk into his flesh to the hilt, penetrating through the back of his neck. Thick blood spurted from both sides as Gus's enormous body fell to the floor. Nearly out of breath, Steve bent over to peer into his face.

He was smiling.

Steve ran over to Brenda, who was now hanging onto the edge of the door and shuffled out into the hallway and into his own apartment. He gently sat her down on the couch, staring into her glazed eyes. Choking sorrow blinded by tears, poured from his own eyes as he embraced her with a love he never gave before. A love that would never leave her. Never forsake her. He laid his head on her lap. "I'm so sorry," he said, tears running down his face. "I'll never leave you alone again. You hear me? I'll never leave you alone again."

He felt her soft hand gently fall on top of his head. His head no longer moved up and down with her breathing, because it stopped. He looked up into her face. "I love you."

Light Entertainment

Hugh McStay

H ugh McStay is a native of Glasgow, Scotland, where he writes avidly in the hopes of scaring and entertaining in equal measure. Recently published in the Thuggish Itch: Theme Park anthology, Hugh has published several short horror tales while his novel gestates in the darker recesses of his mind... Hugh can be found on twitter @angryscotsman81 where he would love to hear from you, and promises that he isn't all that angry.

Devlin was in the business of killing.

But he had never been instructed to murder someone with the lights on.

It was by no means impossible; but it would add a new layer of trickery to an already difficult task. Taking a man's life, no matter how often it was required, was never a simple job. But Mr. Butterscotch, the man who had hired Devlin for the contract, had been very specific about the lights being on during the deed. Specific to the point of fixation.

"Mr. Hamilton should be killed under the bright lights, Devlin," he had said, the words smoothly sliding out of his wide, Cheshire-cat mouth. "After everything he has done, after the crimes he has committed, we want him to see his own demise coming."

The identity of the target only added to the strangeness of the request: Philip Hamilton. Just 'Phil' to a generation of millions on children's television and daytime quiz shows. His TV shows were terrible, but to call them a crime may have been hyperbole.

That Butterscotch had found Devlin at all was a surprise. Throughout his career as a contract killer, he had worked almost exclusively for the Blackmore crime family. His foray into subcontracting had always proved lucrative, but he did not like being surprised by an unwelcome guest in his own home.

"I prefer to do things face to face Mr. Devlin," he had purred. "And you come with a wonderful reputation for dealing with.... unusual cases."

"I don't discuss past jobs with strangers," he said, his mind slitting back to the nightmare he had encountered in the tunnel. "And I don't kill outside the criminal fraternity Mr. Butterscotch. Even the worst of us have codes we don't break."

"Then you are just the man I am looking for," Butterscotch had replied.

And so Devlin now found himself standing on the far side of Phil Hamilton's estate. Pushing through a thicket of branches and leaves in the estate's overgrown hedges, Devlin softly entered Hamilton's property. The mansion sat in the middle of enormous grounds, a stone cathedral to opulence and wealth that had been left to ruin; the windows were murky with filth, the grass of the lawn overgrown and matted, thistles and weeds springing from the ground like unwanted guests at a house party. The driveway, once full of expensive cars and motorbikes, now sat empty and broken, pot-holes running up and down its length like the face of a spotty teenager.

The mansion could have been mistaken for a derelict, fit for nothing but the wrecking ball had it not been for the bright, artificial light that bathed it in an unnatural glow. Tall security lights had been attached to the building carelessly, the iron rivets holding them in place tearing through Victorian artistry. At spaces of ten feet across, twenty feet away from the house, tall steel-poles stood erect with bright security lights facing towards the house, creating a circle of artificial daylight.

Moving slowly and deliberately, Devlin passed through the tall grass. There would be no hiding in the bright circle beyond the lawn, but a quick survey found that there were no guards to be avoided, no cameras to skirt around. He hurried round to the rear of the mansion and stumbled on an item concealed in the grass. Stooping to his knees, he reached down and picked up the item that had almost felled him; a small, dirty-white child's trainer. The clumpy, black grime on the shoe was familiar to Devlin, a stain he had seen on many bodies he had long left to rot. Looking across the thick grass, Devlin saw more discarded items of clothing, each far too small to be worn by an adult, far too bloody to belong to a living being.

"Bastard," Devlin muttered to himself, his resolve doubling at his grim discovery.

Devlin made his way further through the tall grass to the side entrance. Feeling the insides of his jacket, he caressed the leather of his weapon holsters against his shirt. He had no doubt the weapons were still there, but it was a tick he had picked up many years ago that he had convinced himself to be lucky. Turning the door-handle, Devlin smiled as it gently clicked open.

The corridor inside led to the main foyer; a wide reception hall that would have at one time played host to celebrity parties full of captains of industry and heads of television across the UK. It stood empty now, its once immaculate floors covered in years of dirt and filth, broken glass crunching under Devlin's feet as he moved towards the stairs. The walls were potted with cracks and holes, as though someone had been using a sledgehammer to try and kill a scurrying spider.

Ascending the stairs, Devlin's feet squelched on the sodden carpet. The pictures on the wall were a villain's row of celebrity faces who were now in the dock, their public image as broken as the glass frames in which they were trapped; Children's TV presenters with their arms around Phil, his trademark tank-tops in each picture as colourful as the rainbow; politicians, both local and national, who had long faded into obscurity or disgrace; justice had come calling and found them all wanting.

At the top of the stairs, a commemorative golden record for Phil's Comic Relief charity single "Bounce, Bounce, Bounce" sat in a dusty and cracked frame. Devlin remembered the catchy parody song and its annoying music video that seemed to be on every channel for months. It was the kind of infectious earworm that would ruin your day once it had burrowed its way into your brain.

Murdering this bastard was becoming more palatable by the second.

Reaching the top of the stairs, Devlin stood perfectly still and listened. The corridor ahead had several doors running down each side, but from the far away door at the end of the hall, he could hear the dull muffled sound of a television playing. Walking down the blindingly bright hallway, Devlin's senses entered into the heightened state that they often did when he was called into action, guiding him to the solid flooring, avoiding all creaky and loose boards. He stopped before the door, his eyes following his nose to a doorway on his left; a powerful stench of sweet-smelling rot wafted from the room beyond, grabbing Devlin's attention like a child's cry.

The room was the only home in the house to darkness. Stepping inside, Devlin could see that the large double windows at the far end of the room were covered with large wooden slats, nailed immovably in place. Like the rest of the house, there were no furnishings in the room, the carpet design was invisible beneath the filth and grime. Scattered around the room lay torn and bloody clothes, with chunks of flesh that had gone to maggoty ruin splattered across the place like an animal's habitat.

In his many years, Devlin had seen unspeakable horrors and had confronted monsters of all shapes and sizes. But it had been a long time since he had been confronted by something that had found such utter revulsion within him.

"I couldn't help it," came a voice behind him.

Devlin turned to address the figure. The shape was still recognisably Phil Hamilton, the cuddly face of children's entertainment and day-time television monotony. But the bubbly energy that his televisual personality had exuded had been replaced with a foul, greasy lethargy. His usually well-trimmed beard was now shaggy and unkempt, a rat's nest of filth and knots. Devlin could smell his foulness above the pungent scent of death, a once bright yellow tank-top was now a dull breeding ground of germs and feculence.

"Aye, well, I'm here now. You don't need to worry about it anymore," Devlin offered, advancing on him.

Phil turned and walked back to the room he had come from, barely interested in Devlin's presence. Devlin followed him, eager to be rid of his task.

The room beyond contained a large, torn lounge chair. It sat in the middle of a room as lost to ruin as the rest of the house, with a large television was bolted to the wall. The TV was blaring out Youtube clips of Phil's career; interviews with pop stars of the eighties, Phil smiling warmly as children sat around him like lambs in the lion's cage.

"I loved being part of their lives. Watching their faces light up when I came on set, getting their hugs," Phil said.

Devlin reached into his jacket and undid the clip on his left-sided holster.

"I loved them. And they loved me too," Phil continued, his voice barely a whisper. "I thought it was a fair deal. You know? Everything I did was golden, almost a quarter of a century on top. Did you ever watch Phil's Saturday Night Party? Fifteen-million viewers at our peak! Did you ever watch it?"

"I can't say I did," Devlin lied.

Phil's manic smile faded.

"Really? That's disappointing. I think that was some of my best work," Phil said.

"I liked your quiz show," Devlin said.

"Telly Wise?" Phil asked, his face alight like a child on Christmas morning.

"That's the one," he replied. "I assume you know why I'm here, Phil?"

"Yes. I suppose I do. I reneged on the arrangement, I accept that. Mr. Butterscotch?" Phil asked.

"The very one. Bit of an odd character, isn't he?" Devlin replied.

"You have no idea," Phil said, the light in his eyes beginning to retreat to a far-away place inside. "I suppose he told you to keep the lights on?"

The pit of Devlin's stomach felt as though it had dropped from his body.

Something wasn't right.

"Yeh," Devlin said, every muscle in his body beginning to tense.

"I gave everything to those shows. I put my all into everything I ever did. I mean, light entertainment has a certain ceiling, but I like to think that I left people happy?" he uttered, standing from his filth-encrusted comfy chair. "It takes a toll on you. You have to keep them happy though, otherwise, they send men like you."

"Honestly Phil? I have no idea why he wants you dead," Devlin replied, his mind's eye conjuring the tattered and bloody child's shoe. "But I know why I do".

"That's fair. I did awful things for my fame. It's funny how much I wanted the notoriety, the limelight, the spotlight those shows gave me. I think I'd give anything for the light to be dimmed just a tad now," he said softly, jittering like a junkie on a heroine purge. "I'd give almost anything to change things."

"It's a touch late for that," Devlin said, closing the door behind him.

"Do you know how many it takes? I mean, at first, it was just one here or there. But as the years went on, they'd start bringing more and more to my house. Butterscotch liked to watch; he took such joy in it. He would tell me that their flesh would keep me where I was, that their sacrifice would keep fortune on my side. And that their souls would pay for everything else."

"Uh-huh," Devlin said, thankful for his concealed weapons. The years in the televisual wilderness had clearly done a number on Phil's grasp of reality. Although, given what he had seen over the years, reality itself was a fickle thing.

"And since I've stopped, I've had to live in this fucking prison. I can't leave this chamber of light, I can't. It takes over in the dark, without the food to keep it in check," Phil said, walking back and forth like a death row inmate realising that his time was up.

Phil took off his tank-top, revealing a vest underneath that may at one point long ago have been white. He unbuckled his belt and let his jeans drop to the floor, his underwear torn and flimsy.

"I'm really sorry pal, I'm not ready to go yet," Phil said.

"I don't think what's about to happen here is what you're expecting," Devlin said.

"I don't think I'm the one who's in for a surprise," Phil replied, letting his tattered underwear drop to the floor.

Phil Hamilton's member flopped uselessly between his legs like the last hotdog in the jar. The sight of day-time television's former golden boy flashing his unmentionables distracted Devlin from Phil's left hand momentarily, in which he now held a small silver cylinder with a black button on top.

"A bomb?" Devlin asked, scoping the window behind his targets back, mentally calculating the fall.

"Nothing so dramatic," Phil cooed. "The generator trip switch."

With a soft click, the house was plunged into complete darkness.

And with it, the veil of normality was torn asunder.

The air in the room began to heat, the swift change in temperature stealing Devlin's breath from his lungs. The space around Phil began to move and to distort, as though the air itself was tearing open. Phil began to thrash where he stood, foaming at the mouth and gurgling madly. Devlin's eyes had long become accustomed to working in the dark, but the writhing madness before him made him doubt that his senses were working as they should.

Phil's body was contorting, snapping and bending; dozens of tiny hands began to tear from his flesh, pressing their way out of their human prison. Both of his arms now looked like fat, black cacti, the pricks twitching as they pushed their way, elbow length, out of his forearms. His legs began to sprout other, smaller legs, covered in gungy black blood. Phil dropped to his knees and let out a long, cacophonous howl. Worse yet was Phil's body; eyes of every colour began to open across his chest weeping tears and blood in equal measure; his torso began to slit and split open in small, painful cuts; it wasn't until those cuts began to scream that Devlin realised that they were mouths.

Children's voices cried out in pain and terror, too many for Devlin to discern any one message, but enough to recognise the cries for mummies and daddies, the pleas for help.

Dropping to all fours, Phil raised his head to face Devlin. His features, still smug and chirpy, sat above a distended jaw full of carnivorous fangs. Fangs that dripped lustily with saliva, ominously bared at Devlin.

The fear and adrenaline coursing through Devlin's veins braced him against Phil's powerful pounce. The weight of the creature, the combined power of its many hands, pushed Devlin to the ground and pinned his arms. Devlin felt the cold touch of the many-fingered limb as the screams continued. Looking into the maw of the former television personality, Devlin's brain flashed a memory through his head in a split second; of the last time he confronted the impossible; of the night in the Clyde Tunnel, when the dark angel had come for him; the pain he felt as she wrenched him from his car, her enormous wingspan blocking out everything else in his field of vision; of the smell of sulphur on her burning, ancient body.

And of how she too had made the same error in judgement as 'Phil' had; to underestimate him.

"I actually don't know what will happen when I devour you, I'm kind of interested to find out," Phil growled, smiling.

Wrenching with all his strength, Devlin freed his right hand from Phil's grip and placed it inside his coat. As his hand gripped the hilt of his dagger, Phil bit into his shoulder. Screaming, Devlin pulled the dagger from the holster and slashed it across Phil's many-eyed chest. Recoiling, blood and pus pouring down his chest, Phil screeched in pain. Devlin pushed himself quickly to his feet. Considering his options, pain, and planning vying for his attention in equal measure, Devlin decided that there was only one course of action open to him.

The creature advanced on him, stalking him on all fours like a beast from the jungles of hell. Gritting his teeth as blood poured down his arm, Devlin prayed his maths was correct.

Leaping over its head, Devlin's right foot found purchase on the creatures back as he pushed off towards the far away window. Flying through the air, Devlin covered his face with his forearm as he crashed through the glass. The ground rushed towards him like an oncoming truck, and he landed with a crunching bounce as the glass crashed around him. Pulling himself gingerly to his feet, Devlin could feel his ribs moving in his chest like loose kindling, the pain in his shoulder now fighting it out with a new companion for attention. He looked up to see Phil's grotesque and twisted form pulling itself over the window ledge.

Running from the house, Devlin ran as though the devil himself were on his heels. His arm hung limp and useless by his side as the blood continued to pour from the creature's bite, the cool night air turning to fire in his lungs. His every breath was now an act of defiance, his every step an affront to the natural laws. Devlin could hear Phil gaining on him from behind, the man-beast pounding after him on all fours. The never-ending screaming of the children trying to be heard over the growling of the creature that had consumed them. Bursting from the long grass, Devlin charged head-first through the thicket of bushes he had so cautiously passed through upon entry, the twigs scratching his face as he broke through.

Overhead, the screaming, contorted form that was partly Phil Hamilton flew past and landed twirling, several feet in front of him. Devlin dropped to his knees; the chase was over.

Phil prowled back and forth like a tiger playing with its prey, his welcoming eyes never leaving Devlin's own.

"That blade you used, nothing should be able to cut me when I am ready to feed..." Phil growled above the voices.

"I've had it a long, long time," Devlin replied, panting.

"Where did you get it?" Phil asked.

"Germany. Long before you became whatever the fuck it is you are," Devlin said, panting hard.

"I really had stopped. But you wouldn't let me be," Phil grunted, advancing slowly.

"I got one other thing in Germany too," Devlin said, reaching into his pocket. "My car."

Clicking the bottom button of his car keys, two powerful LED headlights burst into life from the gloom behind Phil. The bright light exposed the monstrosity in its full form, the children's screams silenced as the slits in his torso closed, their eyes receding back into the black and their limbs returning to their flesh prison. Phil cried in agony as the transformation reversed, his humanity regaining control of his body.

"I really wanted to stop," he whimpered as Devlin approached.

"I know," he replied, thrusting his ancient blade into Phil's blackened heart. Whatever remained of Phil's soul escaped from him with a breathless whimper, his eyes staring into the distance.

Devlin pulled the dagger from Phil's heart and wiped the blood on his coat before sliding it back into his holster. As he did so, his phone began to softly vibrate in his pocket.

"Hello?" he asked, holding the phone to his ear.

"Excellent work Mr. Devlin, the money will be in your account within the hour," came Butterscotch's voice.

"How did you know I'd finished?" he asked.

"Because he's with us now, Mr. Devlin."

"Who are you, Mr. Butterscotch?" Devlin asked. "Did you make him take those children?"

An uneasy silence hung on the phone.

"You don't want to believe everything you hear, Mr. Devlin. I just called to say thank you, and to tell you not to worry about the clean-up. It will be taken care of," Butterscotch replied.

The phone went dead in Devlin's hand, the unforgiving tone of the disconnected line humming incessantly in his ear. Devlin could already feel his broken ribs knitting themselves back together, the oozing bite wound on his shoulder had almost closed completely. Wiggling his fingers, the feeling returning to them slowly, he admired the chaos that he had survived with a smile.

"Be seeing you, Mr. Butterscotch," Devlin said, throwing his phone into the long grass.

"Be seeing you."

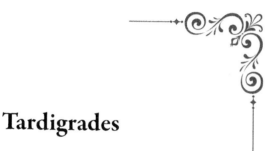

Tardigrades

Mike Sherer

My screenplay 'Hamal_18' was produced in Los Angeles and released direct to DVD, and is available to purchase at Amazon or to rent at Netflix DVD. My mystery/fantasy novel 'A Cold Dish' was published by James Ward Kirk Fiction and is available at Amazon in paperback and digital format. 'Tardigrades' is the 14th short story of mine to have been published, along with four novellas. My travel blog 'American Locations' is posted weekly on my web site: http://www.mikesherer.word-press.com.[1]

---

1. http://www.mikesherer.wordpress.com./

The monstrosity on my left shoulder terrified me. Although I only got a glimpse of the horror in the mirror before it disappeared, its image was seared into my brain. I gripped the bathroom sink screaming, afraid to touch it, to attempt to knock it off, afraid even to move.

Then it disappeared. Leaving me quaking, with legs too weak to support me. I slid down to the floor. Immediately I checked my left shoulder, now that I could no longer see its reflection in the mirror, to make sure it didn't come back. It didn't. My scream had apparently scared it away.

My scream also brought my wife running. She found me sitting on the bathroom floor in my underwear, trembling, searching madly across my body for anything that shouldn't be on it. "What happened?!"

"Do you see anything on me?"

"Like what?"

"Like a monster."

She gave me a quick scan. "Of course not. Did you get a shock?"

The shock she was referring to was to have come from the pacemaker/defibrillator recently implanted in my chest below my left shoulder. "No." I paused to consider. Could that have been what happened? My heart rhythm got out of whack and the device produced an electric shock to force it back into rhythm. But I hadn't felt anything. My cardiologist had warned me it was like the kick of a mule. Yet I had felt nothing. I looked sheepishly up at my worried wife. Was she worried for my sanity? "Help me up." Taking her hand, I gripped the sink with my other and rose to my feet.

"What's this talk about monsters?"

I shook my head as she led me on unsteady legs to our bed. "I don't want to talk about it. I've got to calm down. The way my heart is racing I might get a shock from the defibrillator after all."

She helped me to stretch out. "Just relax. It's Saturday. There is nothing urgent we have to do. Jim's game isn't until two. If you don't feel up to it we won't go."

She was referring to our grandson and his soccer game. "I should be okay by then." I closed my eyes. But I could still see it. A grey leathery barrel with eight legs, at the ends of which were long sharp claws. But the worst feature was its face. Because there wasn't one. At the front where a face should have been the barrel tapered down to a small circular opening. Neither Poe nor Lovecraft could have dreamed up such a terror. Even worse, I had felt it. Those claws had dug into my shoulder to gain purchase on me. And that round gaping hole in front had been reaching toward my neck. To do what? To feed on me? I felt all over my left shoulder and that side of my neck. I could discover no injuries. It had not pierced the skin. My scream had frightened it away.

I went to the soccer game, but I couldn't stop thinking about it. I kept feeling my left shoulder to reassure myself it hadn't returned. My wife seated next to me kept a wary watch. "What's wrong with your shoulder?" I merely shook my head and tried not to act crazy. "Is something wrong with your device?"

That floored me. I had not made the connection. The thing had appeared on my left shoulder, directly above where the device was implanted. It had only been little over a month since the procedure. The heart attack I had suffered had been a minor one and had done no lasting damage. The problem with my heart was electrical. The signals that controlled the rhythm of my heartbeat were getting scrambled. The pacemaker/defibrillator would help keep the signals regular, and in the event my heartbeat accelerated to a dangerous rate the device would automatically shock it back to its normal pace. The device was always on, monitoring my heartbeat. Could it cause me to hallucinate? But I had felt the thing perched on my shoulder. Can you feel a hallucination?

After the soccer game, I scanned the manual that came with the device. No mention of hallucinations. I got online and checked several forums. No one had ever experienced hallucinations after having the device installed. So I could write that off as a cause of my unholy visitation.

Yet how had I conceived such a monstrosity? Can you hallucinate something you have no knowledge of? I could not recall ever having seen anything remotely like what had been about to latch its sucker-like mouth onto my neck. Where had that image come from? What was that thing?

I undertook more Internet searches. Eventually, I found an image of my horror. Tardigrades. Also known as water bears or moss piglets. It was a micro-animal. Its normal size was 0.5 mm, or 0.02 inch when fully grown. The creature I had seen was nearly a foot. And they were practically indestructible. They had been found all over the Earth, in every environment. From mountaintops to the deep sea and mud volcanoes, from tropical rain forests to the Antarctic. Tardigrades were among the most resilient known animals, able to survive extreme conditions that would be rapidly fatal to nearly all other known life forms, such as exposure to extreme temperatures, extreme pressures both high and low, air deprivation, radiation, dehydration, and starvation. Tardigrades had even survived exposure to outer space. In other words, what had attacked me was practically indestructible.

The next time I saw one was in the middle of the night. I was sound asleep in bed. I sleep in my undershorts, so I was bare-chested. And I usually sleep on my back. I was tugged out of a deep sleep by a sucking sensation. I opened my eyes to see the thing perched on my chest with its horrid circular mouth attached to my left nipple. I screamed and flailed wildly with all four limbs. This time the tardigrade didn't disappear. Its round mouth-like opening had some kind of teeth sunk into me and it was sucking something out of me. I whacked it with a wild swing, sending it flying across the room. But it disappeared before hitting the wall.

It didn't disappear into the dark. It actually disappeared. There was a device under my bed that emitted a green glow. This device had a wireless connection to the device implanted in my chest. It recorded my heart activity and broadcast the information to my cardiologist. So the room was dimly lit. The monster didn't disappear into the gloom. It disappeared in mid-air.

But I had touched it this time. It had felt squishy. Its body had given softly to my blow. And my chest had hurt when I knocked it off. It had been latched onto me. Obviously feeding, like a mosquito. But feeding on what? I knocked the light on my nightstand over while trying to turn it on.

My wife turned hers on. "Are you having a nightmare?"

I saw a circular pattern of small puncture wounds around my left nipple. "Can a nightmare do this?" I asked her.

She bent down for a close look. "What happened to you?"

"The monster came back. And it was feeding on me. Like a mosquito."

I jumped out of bed. But my wife wasn't budging, not until I made sure that thing wasn't hiding somewhere. I searched every corner of our master bedroom, under the bed and all the other furniture, in the closets, in the master bath. It was gone. Only then would she get up. We turned on every light in the house and searched everywhere. The tardigrade was truly gone. But to where?

As the dawn sun crept up we were seated at the kitchen table with coffee. "Maybe it's still here," I suggested. That brought a scowl to my wife's sleep-deprived early morning face. "It's a micro-animal. Normally we'd never see it. It's tiny. It could still be here and we'd never know it." My wife drew her feet up off the floor and tucked them under her butt. "There could be hundreds of them here right now and we just can't see them."

"Shut up!"

She wanted to ignore the thing. But I couldn't. It hadn't been feeding on her. So it was back to the Internet. The first reassuring thing I learned was they were prevalent in mosses and lichen. As far as I knew our house was moss-free. So more than likely we weren't infested with them. The second reassurance Google gave me was they fed on plant cells, algae, and small invertebrates. So why had this one been feeding on me?

I saw my doctor the next day. As soon as I bared my chest he cracked a joke. The little punctures were in a perfect circle around a nipple. He wanted to know what kind of kinky sex play my wife and I had engaged in. I assured him she wasn't the perpetrator, that something had bitten me. So blood was drawn for testing, to see if any infection had resulted from the bite. The blood tests turned up negative. The bite hadn't seriously injured me in any way. My doctor told me to keep an eye on it, to make sure it didn't become infected. And to lay off the kinky stuff. He did not believe it was a bite mark.

I can't blame him. I went back on the Internet to study bite patterns. The only thing that might have made such a circular pattern was some kind of eel. Or a monstrously huge tardigrade.

Later that day I got a call from my cardiologist's office. They wanted me to come in immediately, they were getting some unusual readings from my device. My wife insisted on driving me. The tardigrade showed up in the car. When she saw it in the rearview mirror crawling up the back of my seat she screamed and nearly wrecked before pulling over on the side of the Interstate. Guessing right away what was happening, I lunged forward and turned around. It was perched on the top of my seat. I punched it as hard as I could. Then leaned over my seat, expecting to find it in the back seat or on the floor and hoping to finish it off. But it was gone.

My wife was out of the car. "What is that thing?!"

"A tardigrade."

Before I could elucidate further, a police car pulled up behind us with its lights flashing. It was a good thing my wife was too upset to talk, it gave me an opportunity to lie. I didn't want to be sent to the loony bin, which the officer might have done if he heard the truth. I told him I'd had an episode with my heart and been shocked. Witnessing it had so upset my wife she had pulled off. I told him the defibrillator had just been recently implanted and this was the first episode I'd had. I showed him the medical I.D. card I'd gotten from the device manufacturer. Once assured my wife was calm enough he let us go, on the condition she drove. He didn't believe I should be drive if I was getting electrical shocks.

My wife wasn't ready to get back in the car. As the officer walked back to his car, she peered in the driver's window at me. From a safe distance. "Where did that thing go?"

"I don't know."

"Is it still in the car?"

"I don't see it. Do you?" She looked into the back. "Get in."

"Look under the seats."

I glanced back at the patrol car. The officer was impatiently waiting for us to pull out. "We've got to go, honey."

"Look under the seats!"

I unbuckled, opened my door and dropped to my knees outside the car to peer under the seats. "It's not under here. It's gone."

Raising back up, I saw the officer climbing back out of his car. So I lied again. "She lost her phone."

"Find it later. You need to go. It's not safe here on the side of the Interstate."

I looked across the car at my wife. "He's going to arrest us if we don't drive away." At last, she made a move toward her door. I smiled and waved at the officer, then climbed in. He waited next to his car until my wife finally crept in behind the wheel. His lights had been flashing the whole time, so now as he climbed back in his patrol car he flipped on his siren to alert passing motorists that we were pulling out.

"I'm shaking so bad I feel like I'm going to pass out," my wife said as she started the car.

"Just drive to the next exit and we'll pull over somewhere and search the car high and low. Okay? But we have to go now."

At long last, she pulled out. The officer pulled out behind us, turning off his lights and sirens as we sped up. We took the first exit we came to, and the police car went on. We pulled off to the side at a gas station at the top of the exit ramp. My wife hopped out of the car before the engine died. I'd never seen her move so fast.

I poked high and low, even opened the trunk and tore through that. Nothing. "Where did it go!?" she demanded.

"I don't know. But that's what it does. It disappears into thin air." The way she was quaking I was afraid she would still yet pass out. "Why don't you take a taxi back home? I can drive to my appointment."

"With that thing in the car?"

"It's not in the car anymore. I looked." It didn't take much to persuade her. She was not getting back into our car.

Once I put her in a taxi, I drove on to see my cardiologist. He said my device was acting in a way he'd never seen before. The signal it was broadcasting was way too powerful. He made a few adjustments, which he accomplished through a wireless connection. Then he said I was good to go. I asked him what could have caused the problem, and what this particular problem could cause to happen. In other words, I was asking about the monster without mentioning it. He said although my case was unusual, it was no big deal, that these devices often needed to be fine-tuned after being implanted. He told me the problem had been dealt with and I shouldn't worry about it.

I was still worried. I called a nephew who specialized in cancer research, and he agreed to see me. This had nothing to do with cancer, but my nephew had a degree in biology and might know something about tardigrades. My wife sounded relieved when I called to say I'd be late. She didn't even ask what the doctor had said, she had other things on her mind. I didn't think I'd be sleeping with her for a while.

My nephew didn't believe me. He said micro-animals couldn't grow to a giant size, like the one I'd seen. Also, there was no way a malfunctioning pacemaker/defibrillator could do such an incredible thing. Besides, my house or car wasn't the kind of environment they preferred. When I insisted I had read they could exist anywhere, even in outer space, he conceded the point. When asked where it could have gone, he said if it could grow to such dimensions there was no reason why it couldn't shrink back to its original size. That could be why it seemed to disappear. Also, since it had appeared both in my house and in my car, there was a good chance I was carrying the thing on my body.

That sure didn't make me feel any better. But he said it was really nothing to worry about. My body, in fact, the entire world, was overrun by micro-organisms. He pulled up highly-magnified horrific images from the Internet of micro-animals. Dust mites that looked like shaggy sheep infested houses, especially beds, and ate the dead skin that flaked off my body. He said more than likely I slept with millions of them on my pillow. A springtail, looking like a rabbit from Hell, could leap one-hundred times its body length and infested the soil. There could be millions of these in my lawn. A velvet mite, looking like a giant spider from a fifties science fiction B-flick, was another denizen of my lawn.

When he showed me an image of a moth caterpillar I'd had enough. I had seen enough horrors to power my nightmares for the rest of my life. Although he assured me these creatures were so small I'd never see them and that most of them were harmless to humans, except for maybe causing a rash, I felt worse than when my nephew had first greeted me. I thanked him for his time and fled, determining to stay on my sidewalk and driveway, never to set foot on my lawn again.

The world was filled with horrific monstrosities. Not being able to see them made their existence even more frightening. These little demons could be, probably were, crawling across my flesh every moment of my life. Why would God create such grotesqueries? Now that I had seen images of these abominations I couldn't unsee them. I could practically feel their tiny hairs and feelers everywhere on my body as they roamed across my flesh. And one, a tardigrade, could somehow grow to near-human dimensions to feed on me. Maybe it was swelling to an incredible size the way a tick swells after ingesting its fill of blood.

I and my wife slept apart. She took the guest bedroom since the transmitting device for my pacemaker/defibrillator was set up under our bed. The tardigrade never reappeared. If something in the unique signal from my device had affected it, once my device was adjusted by the cardiologist it never came back. At first, my wife wouldn't even get near me. But with time the memory of the horror she had seen in the car faded. After a month she was able to hug me without trembling with revulsion. But sleep with me? Not yet.

When I awoke one night with the tardigrade's claws at the ends of its eight legs affixed to my chest and its horrid circular mouth latched onto my left nipple, sucking away, I forced myself to remain calm. There had to be a way to kill it before it could shrink back to its normal size and hide somewhere on my body. Barely containing my fright, I cast a desperate gaze about the green-hued room for a weapon within reach. That's when I saw the others. On the bed, on the floor, my nightstand, my dresser, the chest of drawers. All the horrors my nephew had shown me, and many he hadn't, grown to the size of the tardigrade, creeping, crawling, slinking, slithering about. All awaiting their turn. At me. A feeler slipped into my ear. A hair tickled my eyes. Something nosed inside my undershorts to nibble on my genitals. I was frozen in terror, unable to draw a breath. Until a springtail leaped up from the floor and landed on my face. Then I screamed.

The next morning the wife walked in to find her husband dead in bed, his body riddled with bite and claw marks. His death was ruled a heart attack. Even with all the wounds on his body. They were all superficial, and no toxins or infections as a result of these strange injuries turned up in the autopsy. Although there were several unusual rashes at different places, even those were nothing that could have killed him. The strangest thing was how the pacemaker/defibrillator's battery was drained. As if it had been sucked dry. It must have been defective. That was why the device hadn't been able to stave off the heart attack that had killed him.

But his widow knew what had really happened. She was institutionalized after clawing much of her skin off with her fingernails, raving about monsters crawling all over her body and how she had to get them off her. The attending physician realized her mind had snapped. Yet was intrigued by how she could have self-inflicted the ring of punctures around her left nipple.

For the Dolls Had Eyes
A Tale of the Bajazid

Kenneth Bykerk

K enneth lives and writes in the ghost town suburb of an Arizona ghost town. The places he played as a child still serve to inspire, but in ways that the child of yore would probably be disturbed by. That kid was a scaredy-cat.

There once was a witch who did not want to be alone. However strange as this may sound, however odd it may be to the Casual Reader, it must be remembered that a witch is not unlike any other born of woman and sired by man. They experience happiness and joy, sadness and loss; the whole range of emotions that are possible to this frail and imperfect form. That one is a witch does not preclude them from those base desires and fears which exalt and shame. They suffer, as do all, the afflictions of the soul, those singular traits which set mankind apart from the beasts without tongue. The Children of Adam, be they of Eve or of Lilith dark, are bound one and all to the daemons of their own design, patterns predictable to the Phrenologist's touch. Each and every soul upon the earth holds these truths, known and unknown, and they represent in myriad ways, shaped by predestination and circumstance. With this said, it should come as no surprise that even a witch could fear being alone.

Of the phobias that plague, to each their own weight and importance are placed by those who suffer them. The arachnophobe will set her fear of spiders far above practical cautions even to the point of self-endangerment while the acrophobe will go to any lengths to avoid a height. No amount of candles can ever assuage the concerns of the nyctophobic and those suffering claustrophobia should never dig for gold in the depths of the Earth. Not all fears though are based external and thus overcome through judicious avoidance. There are those anxieties whose origins stem from deep within the psyche and have no place, no manifestation in the physical world. For these elusives, no representations exist outside the shadows that steal the certainties of sanity. Whether the concoction be the pharmacist's juice and powdered leaves or the witches' herbs and gathered roots, alleviations exist in some form or another, even if poured from a bottle, for many of the most common reservations. No such potion exists, however, to alleviate the eternal isolation of eremophobia.

Not always does the Paranoid fear needlessly nor the Hypochondriac imagine their ails. Sometimes the hunt truly is on and sometimes the evidence is in a bloody chunk coughed up. There exists as well the possibility that one might be of such loathsome nature and unpleasant personality that no others do truly wish to associate with them, even those of closest intent. From earliest memory to the obsession of her doom, the Patchwork Witch sought with desperation acceptance yet ever she felt denied. In the associations she had known throughout her life, from the coven that raised her to the many such circles and klatches she passed through over the years, she felt always she was unwelcome and did not belong. That her presence would sooner than later serve to render her companionship distasteful was a truth exasperating her sense of isolation and the existential fear which lay beneath. She knew the loneliness of the outcast and longed to belong.

The arguments of nature and nurture combine to compel witness a life lived in desperate desire to belong yet fearing no such place existed. She was born under a caul during the abandonment of the moon, March of 1839. The midwife attending, an experienced hag of strong reputation, saw the portents and safely peeled that skin from the baby's skull, whispering to her two young apprentices the importance of their find in short, coded hisses. The caul was auspicious, a sign of fortune and prosperity, a predestination assigned at birth by the forces beyond and the eclipse held meanings vast in range. As that cap came off, revealed beneath was a birthmark of distinct proportions and the midwife hissed in surprise. A strawberry scar traced the left half of the baby's scalp, running from the back of her neck to end, a swooping, jagged hook connecting eye to nostril. Another blemish, one deeper port and shaped in crescent descending, sat above the left eye.

The mother lasted four hours, her hemorrhaging internal and unstoppable. The husband, a quarry-man, was allowed in to spend what time there was that remained. His heart was broken and the midwife and her daughters treated him with due gentleness and respect. The child, his new-born daughter, was weak, her cries plaintive and desperate. She was not expected long to last. He held his fading loves there in those hours while the three witches cleaned up the remains of the birth and of their crime. When the sun painted its first hopes in the eastern sky, the dying woman, knowing her husband close and touching softly her baby's head, opened her eyes and christened the child with her last sight, her last breath. The infant was quiet not long after and her mother was laid to rest, a small, tightly wrapped bundle against her breast.

For fifteen years, Dawn rose early and worked late, laboring daily those chores needed to run a house. For fifteen years she served without belonging in a house jealously guarded. She learned her trade and craft through witness, through absorption of proximity and awareness. She learned the nature of words and symbols and herbs and roots tending the needs of the coven that held her. They were of a family, the Witches of Keeffe's Point as they were in the end remembered, settled on a deeply forested peninsula of land jutting into a small lake in the Green Mountains of southern Vermont. The midwife was now a woman comfortably mature, her twin daughters, age ten when Dawn was born, now grown into their own. A matriarch, a woman ancient and infirm, shared as well that cabin and was Dawn's principle charge and the reason she was not allowed to leave that peninsula. It was from the senile, old witch Dawn learned most, lessons direct which would infuriate the midwife upon learning of it. The beatings she suffered were regular.

One night, as the work week of men drew to a close and pay circulated among the establishments of the nearby town, the twins and their mother left to collect what they could. This was regular custom, leaving Dawn alone with the old, senile witch while they went off to cavort and live amongst the people whom Dawn had only seen from across the lake. Rebellion wakes the hearts of all who have the fire of life within them at some point. Dawn was fifteen when she put on the dress taken from the twin's wardrobe and stole down the narrow neck that connected the peninsula to land. Eyes wide with awe, she walked through the streets of town wandering ultimately into the establishment anchoring the activities of the night. Her presence in the doorway was unexpected, drawing all eyes upon her. The twins were there as was the midwife, all three gaily wrapping themselves around men with pay in their pockets. All three froze, unbelieving and undone as one man stood forward, his face bloodless and her name on his lips.

Dawn Campbell now had a full name. She was told the man who fell dead before her that night was her father, her mark his remembrance. Questions were raised and the body of a woman long dead unearthed the next day to reveal a small dog interred in her arms. A party of outrage descended upon the peninsula cabin to find vengeance already wreaked in part. The midwife, bloodied and torn, alone remained alive, the twins and the aged crone slain as if by beast unnatural in cruelty. The midwife, eyes rabid and feral, screamed incoherent condemnations at the welp who took her signs from the circle and let in the Beast. As these words were choked off by rope, Dawn could already feel the suspicions of the townsfolk upon her. What signs did she have but those that marked her face? She had risen from the dead, slain her father and freed a beast in one night. No, she did not belong.

Dawn arrived in Baird's Holler in 1873, a small mining town sprung up in the central mountains of the Arizona Territory. Her years following her flight from the mountains of Vermont had taken her throughout the young nation, each stop adding to her lore and further cementing her sense of alienation. Nowhere did she belong and so she went west to lands where she might find a community small enough to need a woman wise in the ways of healing and birth, a place she might be welcomed. Baird's Holler was a hope, a burgeoning place overflowing with wealth and wickedness. It was also one with witches established already, a welcome find for the coven was young and yet small. It was as well respected, ran by the widow of a man who died in the mines saving the lives of others. Her status was raised as was a house built for her, one she converted to a home for widows of the mine. When Dawn arrived on the Bajazid, the Widow Jackson's home, only one year established, had three boarders. Hard-rock mining is dangerous work.

The Witches of the Widow House welcomed Dawn into their circle but not into their coven. Her evident strength, the portents visible to all who could discern clear upon her face, the Widows accepted her friendship for the fortune of association but they would not let her in, let her join their select. This was not at first an issue that vexed her for their friendship and community blinded her to this omission. She went home each night to the shack she let, unconcerned her presence was accepted only so conditionally at the Widow House. She did not question why she was kept at distance until a fourth boarder was admitted into the coven abruptly one evening. She did not visit the Widow House for a week after, keeping her solitude in morose speculation on why she was separate from those gathered in communion. Her fears of rejection tinged her thoughts with the poison of suspicion.

When a fifth widow was admitted to the house, Dawn voiced her concern to Mrs. Jackson. Delores, a kind woman plantation born raised abrupt to wealth and prominence, explained the reason simple and clear. Each of the women who lived under that roof were widows, and not just widows, but of men who had perished or were lost within the mine the town was built around. There was a distinction between perished and lost on the Bajazid, one that Dawn could feel in the energies of the valley. Sometimes men working the mines would vanish, lost in the maze of tunnels dug into the mountain. With rumor of men so lost being seen long after their disappearance beginning to arise amongst those who worked below, this distinction was well made. Not all who died in this place did die deaths that could be determined such. That Dawn understood. Never before had she felt such power as the forces that held sway over this valley. The Widow House, Delores Jackson explained, was bound by these powers. Admittance was payment in blood to the force that held sway over the creek and the valley it carved. The bond of betrothal must be broken.

In late 1875, a sixth widow was invited to the house for permanent communion and Dawn barely held her tongue in jealous disgust. She was still accepted into the Widow House, still befriended by those who dwelt there, but the demeanor of the relationship had changed. A pall had drawn down, a curtain of uncertainty and suspicion disguised by pleasantries uttered insincere. Knowing this poison was determined to destroy at last what it must unchecked, she took the action she knew would most secure her future and her acceptance into this coveted clan. Dawn Campbell got married.

Jack Weaver was a kind man, one known among the community for his forthwith nature and honest dealings. He served as a foreman with the Mortenson Mine, the operation that anchored the town. His crew was the one sought by all miners who worked those tunnels for his fairness, his unswerving dedication to those who worked under him and the honor of working the best production crew in the mine. His virtues were hailed by all, the measure of his character far outweighing any pity felt for the circumstances of his appearance. Where Dawn was born with crescent and scythe seared into her skin, Jack Weaver's deformities were not of birth. It was his years leading Zouave in grey jackets that formed the basis of his command and respect. It was on the fields outside of Antietam where he earned the face that forbid him love. It did not take too much to convince him that only the scarred could see the beauty in scars and soon he took home as bride a woman who saw something more in him than a ruined face. She saw in him a price paid.

For a full year, Jack Weaver lived a life he never thought he would, a blissful repast from the lonely days to which he had been doomed. For a full year, Dawn Weaver continued her charade until she felt that her waiting had been fulfilled. When Jack Weaver collapsed one day in late November of 1876, Dawn was summoned to the offices of the Mortenson Mine to view his remains. Her tears flowed with modest display, keenly aware excess would be unseemly and suspicious in a woman her age married so brief. The company physician had been properly duped and the death was declared failure of the heart under strain of impending age. The Widow Weaver, hailed by some an angel for taking in a man so disfigured and allowing his last months to be a wish fulfilled, donned her weeds and made her way to the house of the Widow Jackson.

Where once she had been a welcome guest, where she had expected to be greeted with commiserating words, she was turned away with withering accusations of murder and treachery. They knew, they claimed, the nature of her craft and her crime. Her protestations of innocence fell upon deaf ears so she turned herself to accusations of the very same, aware fully that not all the men lost to these women were loved. Indeed, Dawn knew that some dooms had been coerced by these very women in order to recruit to their coven. The hypocrite whose house it was laughed in her face and lied that those men had been brutes, rabid beasts needing to be culled lest the women be the ones put through the furnace. Jack Weaver, Dawn replied, was just such a man and her actions, all pretense of innocence tossed aside, were just. Jack Weaver, Delores Jackson declared, was an innocent man, a good man and therefore a death unjustified. His widow was not welcome, neither as a member in full or to ever shadow the stoop of the Widow House again. The threat held the power of seven steeped in knowledge she knew too well. The rejected widow retreated to the house left her and the bitter recriminations of her fears.

That very night the Widow Weaver put in motion her revenge. In her travels of yore, she had absorbed traditions vast, far beyond those who enslaved her youth. Magic is nothing more than drawing links between representation and reality in order to rearrange through will the order of that reality represented. Seven dolls she sewed in the ensuing days and in the weeks that followed, she worked to draw the links that needed to be. Diligence and persistence, along with bribes to the unfortunate and doomed who had come to Baird's Holler to fail, delivered her at last the personal effects needed to complete the now eight dolls that waited her ministrations. On the night of February 29, 1877, Hati gobbled at the moon and swallowed her whole as night fell. The moment at hand, an orgy of violence was released upon the idols representing. The rejected witch slept sound that night amid the wreckage of her enemies' remains, confident and content.

She woke slow, her body aching from dreams sewn by needles cruel. She did not wake in her chair as she had rested after her revenge. Instead, she woke on the floor by the cold hearth, her bones stiff and her clothes marked by hundreds of small reddish-brown stains corresponding to scabbed pricks her body over. Her hunger was ravenous and without further thought, she devoured a half loaf baked the day before but now turning with hints of growth. The hour, she noted, was late in the afternoon but the sleep of a day would not spoil a loaf. Disoriented, she began the process of cleaning the mess of the night before when she at last noticed what shouldn't be. There upon the small divan that anchored the room were eight little dolls lying in a row, repaired down to the button eyes.

Herein began her war, the struggle that consumed her attentions and ultimately, her self. The witches in the Widow House were powerful, a combined knowledge of diverse traditions as the women represented were not monolithic in culture and craft. Nor did the number under that roof stay stagnant but climbed over the years until twelve boarders completed with their hostess a closed circle of thirteen. Delores Jackson and one other brought the traditions born of plantation need, that mix of African belief tinged in Christian hues the Casual Reader will recognize for their use of dolls. The western traditions were covered in full from the fens of Ireland to the wooded hills of the Roma, the ice-bound fjords of the north to the secrets of the Sabbat for the Black Goat of the Pyrenees. These all Dawn had some knowledge of, some familiarity with from her travels. The Berber and Bedouin traditions, the Persian and Hindi and Chinese influences in that house were alien to her, magics related but of different texture and focus than what she knew. Strangest of all to her was the Native woman who hid within that coven, a Navajo widow of a man murdered so her lore could enrich the house. Thirteen witches, a full circle steeped in understandings that combined, far outstripped her own broad craft. Still, she went to war, her jealously and the bitterness of rejection she had faced changing her fear of ostracization to a righteous charge of vengeance.

There is a certain pleasure that comes from hating, a quietude of the soul that soothes the unsettling sensations of ennui. Hate fills the empty spaces left when tenderness dies and hope recedes. It grants purpose to the damned when all else is forsaken, purifying the soul and remaking complete that which had been torn asunder. The Widow Weaver luxuriated in her hatred, basked in the warmth it spread through her shrinking soul. Meticulously and judiciously she planned out the inflictions to be applied and took deep pleasure in their execution. Each night needles pierced the fabric flesh of the dolls and each morning, she woke to wash pin-pricks of blood dried from her skin.

One morning she woke to something new, an alteration made for which she could not account. Her attention was drawn to it by the dull ache it left, a bruising that had no business being there. It was not though a bruise but a stitch that ran the perimeter of a small kite of cloth, a piece she recognized from her collection of scraps. It was sewn directly, this small, pale floral patch, into the very flesh of her calf. She touched the fabric and could feel the enraged meat beneath. She pulled at the stitching tentatively but the pain made her stop. In a rage, she savaged each in turn the then nine dolls she harbored. Satisfied after hours of meticulous torture, she continued her day with a dull ache and a warm glow. That this perversion of her flesh had taken place, sorcery if ever there was, proved then her harassment was working. Any suffering she endured was washed away with this good news.

Each new addition to the Widow House was matched with a small, cloth doll specifically sewn until there were thirteen such rags lying about her small hovel with rips and tears to memorialize their suffering.

The Widow Jackson was the main focus of this ire and the doll representing was always tattered and torn, ripped and abused more than any other. Her first assault, the night she tore seven apart, she questioned. She realized her links had yet been too frail to withstand the fury she had unleashed that night. How the dolls destroyed had been repaired she knew not. It happened, that she knew, but she could not account their return, deciding on not remembering her actions due to fatigue rather than allowing suspicions uncertain to rise. Still, when a doll failed, when the damage done was too much to sustain, she always found the abused figure repaired when she woke.

She, a witch, had been bewitched. The quiet war she waged against the witches in the Widow House was returned in assaults delivered in the depths of somnambulistic trance. Not only would she wake to find dolls too far destroyed returned and repaired, but her own flesh suffered steadily as patch by patch was replaced with scraps culled from cloth around the house. As her alterations begin to appear in places visible, discretion required concealment and isolation. Gloves were worn in public until her hands themselves became the gloves excused and always a darkened widow's veil for blue fleur-de-lis should never appear upon a woman's right cheek. When the scythe upon her left cheek was replaced with scarlet felt and the crescent with burgundy silk, the depth of her disguise required near complete concealment. Such disfigurements though are difficult to fully hide for she still had business she must conduct with the community in which she dwelt, a distasteful undertaking for her fear of isolation had become a desire to be let alone.

Still, she was a witch and in the Valley of Death that was is Bajazid, there were always the desperate who needed services such as she could provide. A tiny few overtime saw the inside of her home and what little word leaked out in rumor whispered always mentioned the presence of dolls lying haphazard and often in state of disrepair. When Delores Jackson heard these rumors, she laughed at the description told for the dolls had eyes. The Casual Reader unknowing might question the significance of buttons sewn onto cloth faces but the Widow Jackson and her witches had plumbed deep and there were secrets which they had learned. There was something dark that dwelt deep within the Bajazid Valley which they all recognized, the same power which the Patchwork Witch herself perceived. The difference was that Dawn never had a tradition to which she belonged, an avatar or god born in darkness to whom she served. The widows of Mrs. Jackson's house all had traditions deep and loa's with whom their spirits communed. Here on the Bajazid those connections were weak if at all and the Widows were able to perceive a hint of That Which Damned.

One truth they understood was that the Dead never left the domain of this cursed valley and their spirits remained restless in impotent agony eternal. When such a spirit forlorn found a figurine, an idol, a child's doll with eyes represented upon its face, that spirit would take refuge within for those shells provided comfort from the agonies of Eternity and the eyes allowed the dead to see. Those of Catholic persuasion often suffered confusions of undignified outrage. The widows in that wicked house laughed for they knew the power of doll magic but they also knew failure when they saw it. Rather than torturing the victims intended, all the Widow Weaver ever accomplished was the torturing of souls already in agony. Revenge becomes an unbreakable circle and the coven in opposition declined the mercy of revealing her mistake.

There is an inescapable curse that comes with hatred, an all-consuming obsession that requires not just revenge but an aggressive proclivity to punish in order to chase that dragon of pleasure lost. Dawn Campbell Weaver got her revenge through the subtle manipulation of a madman. The night the Preacher Jonathan Kearns burned the house of Delores Jackson to the ground with all occupants inside, the Jaguar descended upon the Hunter's Moon and the Patchwork Witch threw all of her dolls into her stove. How many days she slept she did not know but when she woke, thirteen dolls stared back at her and she had no more flesh than her eyes. The ashes at Mrs. Jackson's were cold and the weather had changed.

For four years she lived a recluse, a woman stooped in stature seen only rarely and always draped in full. Those who yet remained in the dying shell of Baird's Holler did their best to deny knowledge of this distasteful hag and only desperation would drive one to her door. When whispers that the crone had button eyes began, all communion with the community ceased regardless the evident madness of the tellers of those tales. No one sane could believe such an impossibility but on the Bajazid, truth is a transcendent thing and sanity matters not. On the morning she woke without eyes, she knew immediate the cure for she had prepared without the anticipation of the dolls. She took the needle with buttonholed and, touching it to the burlap sealing her sight, pressed. She felt every excruciating pull at the thread but at last, through small, enamel saucers, she saw again. Her sustenance by then came exclusive from the vermin she attracted by vegetables she would raise to rot on her floor and no longer did those functions which enslaved her flesh-bound form draw her notice. Her isolation complete within the midst of uncaring rot, she made peace with her rage and ceased the torture of those dolls she believed were the witches her magic had at last consumed.

Her ignorance her hubris, her damnation she sealed. In July of 1889, as she stumped softly around her house in peaceful acceptance of the isolation she had at last come to cherish, she caught a snag while the moon shied in the night. She was in her kitchen when the stitch began to unravel, the thread from her calf aged and worn. No pain attended the tear for there was no flesh beneath to ache. It was weakness brought on by her seeping doom that drew attention to her plight. In panic, she grasped desperately at a cupboard with one hand, hoping to use the other to staunch the flow. A splinter, a great needle splitting from the aging wood, slipped beneath a seam on her thumb and horror twisted the shapeless demands of her countenance. She knew her end and could do naught but watch as her contents poured in tiny grains onto the floor.

It was more than a year before her door was approached by any but at last it was breached by two soldiers the day the town died in madness. They were securing each residence, ensuring all who remained in this infected place be escorted to safety before they cleansed the town with fire. Inside the cabin, they found nothing but rot and decay, the sole occupants thirteen rag dolls seated on cupboards and chairs around an empty patchwork sock of curious design hung from a splinter cruel. It was an unusual relic to find and ultimately it was sold to a collector of such curiosities for ten dollars.

END

Don't miss out!

Visit the website below and you can sign up to receive emails whenever Madness Heart Press publishes a new book. There's no charge and no obligation.

https://books2read.com/r/B-A-IVRH-ZKIY

About the Publisher

Madness Heart Press is dedicated to bringing you quality horror from new and amazing authors. You can find more books, stories and even listen to the Madness Heart Radio Podcast at MadnessHeart.Press

Printed in Great Britain
by Amazon

24374253R00121